No Turning Back!

The professor's voice came through on the walkie-talkie. He said, "I must seriously advise you to turn right around and come back to the space station."

Miss Pickerell was outraged.

"Professor Aceworthy," she said, "if I've come this far to try to prevent another flood in Square Toe County, I'm certainly going to finish the job. I'm climbing up on the satellite right now."

"Miss Pickerell," the professor said, "I don't wish to alarm you. But it is my duty to warn you that your maneuvering gun holds a limited amount of compressed gas. Can you accurately estimate the amount you will need to get back to the space station? You are taking a terrible chance!"

Miss Pickerell's heart stood still. She hesitated, but only for an instant. She reached out her arm, took a firm hold of the hand grips, and pulled herself to the satellite. . . .

Miss Pickerell and the Weather Satellite

by Ellen MacGregor and Dora Pantell
Illustrated by Charles Geer

#2

AN ARCHWAY PAPERBACK
POCKET BOOKS • NEW YORK

All characters in this book are entirely fictitious.

POCKET BOOKS, a Simon & Schuster division of
GULF & WESTERN CORPORATION
1230 Avenue of the Americas, New York, N.Y. 10020

Copyright © 1971 by McGraw-Hill, Inc.

Published by arrangement with McGraw-Hill Book Company
Library of Congress Catalog Card Number: 71-150781

ISBN: 0-671-56027-1

First Pocket Books printing February, 1980

10 9 8 7 6 5 4 3 2 1

Trademarks registered in the United States and other countries.

Printed in the U.S.A.

Contents

Miss Pickerell
and the
Weather Satellite

A Warning from
Mr. Kettelson

Miss Pickerell was sitting at her big white kitchen table drinking a glass of ice cold peppermintade and trying to fill in the *Square Toe Gazette* crossword puzzle. Miss Pickerell liked crossword puzzles. They helped to take her mind off things she did not want to think about. This morning, there was one thing she very definitely did not want to think about. It was the fact that her seven nieces and nephews would be arriving at her peaceful mountain-top farm at any moment now. They would all talk at once and they would remind her of her promise to take them to see the giant laser at the new Square Toe astronomical observatory. Miss Pickerell shuddered.

"I can't imagine what made me promise them to do that," she said to Pumpkins, her large, black cat who was lying on the table and persistently tearing to shreds the corner of the newspaper that was near him. "I must have been feeling a lot better than I do today."

Pumpkins blinked his lazy, yellow eyes and purred.

Miss Pickerell wondered whether it was going to rain. The sky through her wide kitchen window looked a little dark. And the thumb that she had broken last year when she fell off the barnyard ladder was hurting badly. The doctor said she was imagining it when she told him about how the pain always came just before a storm. Miss Pickerell thought that the doctor's statement was ridiculous, though she was much too polite to tell him so. She simply said, "Thank you, Doctor."

Just to make sure about the weather, Miss Pickerell walked over to the telephone that hung on the wall next to her shining, black coal stove and dialed the weather report number.

"The next few days will be very sunny, warm, and clear," the recorded voice announced metallically into her ear. "The temperatures will be . . ."

Miss Pickerell hung up.

"I don't understand it," she said to herself. "I simply don't understand it."

She resolved not to pay any more attention to her thumb. She concentrated instead on finding a three-letter word that meant the beginning of a holiday. It had to be a word with a V in it.

"Why, it's EVE, of course," she said out loud, as she happily tucked a loose hair pin into place and fixed her eyeglasses a little more firmly on her nose. She was putting the first and last letters where they belonged in the puzzle when she heard the knock on the kitchen door.

"Oh, dear," she sighed. She laid aside her pencil, folded up her newspaper neatly, and went to open the door for the children.

But it was Mr. Kettelson, the hardware store man, who stood on the other side. He looked thin and gray and even sadder than usual.

"Why, good morning, Mr. Kettelson," Miss Pickerell said. "Come in and have a

3

peppermintade. I just made some fresh this morning."

"Thank you," Mr. Kettelson said, sitting down at the table and taking the glass that Miss Pickerell offered him. "How is your cow?"

"She's fine, Mr. Kettelson," Miss Pickerell told him. "I put her in the lower pasture this morning. It's cooler there."

"She and I became very good friends that year when we had the flood in Square Toe County," Mr. Kettelson remarked. "Do you recall that time, Miss Pickerell?"

Miss Pickerell nodded. She could feel the goose pimples coming out all over as she remembered the torrents of rain and the houses floating in the streets and the people and the animals trying to climb up the mountain to safety. Sometimes, in the night, she thought of all those who had been washed away before they could make it to the mountain top. Then she couldn't fall asleep.

Mr. Kettelson took a few sips of peppermintade, put his glass down, and cleared his throat. Then he looked Miss Pickerell straight in the eye.

4

"Do you think, Miss Pickerell," he asked, "that we could have that kind of thing happen again?"

"Impossible!" Miss Pickerell said promptly. "These days, we get our weather forecasts a long time in advance. We are prepared for such an emergency. It's all automatic. The predictions are made by weather satellites."

"Humph!" Mr. Kettelson snorted.

"I beg your pardon?" Miss Pickerell asked.

"I might have known," Mr. Kettelson burst out. "I might have known that you'd be on the side of the machines. After all, you've been to Mars and the moon and the bottom of the ocean and I don't know where else. It's only natural that you should think that . . ."

"Mr. Kettelson!" Miss Pickerell interrupted, talking as loud as she could so that Mr. Kettelson would stop and listen. "I never wanted to go to any of those places. They . . . they just happened."

Mr. Kettelson looked down at the table and patted Pumpkins' head.

"I'm sorry," he said. "I'm very nervous this morning."

"You may be working too hard," Miss Pickerell suggested.

"Not at all," Mr. Kettelson replied. "Business is absolutely terrible. Nobody seems to have any money to spend. I bought up a brand new line of pots and pans that I thought would go over big. But . . ."

Mr. Kettelson paused. He sighed deeply. Miss Pickerell gave him another glass of peppermintade. He drank it down in one gulp and stood up.

"I guess I'd better be getting back," he said. "You never know when a customer will come in."

"No, you never do," Miss Pickerell agreed.

"Personally, I think it's going to rain," Mr. Kettelson said, sounding pessimistic again, "and there won't be any customers at all."

"Well," Miss Pickerell told him, trying hard not to think about her thumb and to reassure herself, "I just heard the weather report and . . ."

"And I suppose you are of the opinion that the weather report can never be wrong, Miss Pickerell," Mr. Kettelson interrupted, running his hands excitedly through his few gray hairs and making them stand up all around his face.

"I don't see how it can be," Miss Pickerell said, reflecting about this. "I looked up the way the forecasts are made in my new edition of the encyclopedia. There are two kinds of weather satellites. One kind orbits around the equator of the earth and the other kind around the North and South poles. And the space station that orbits around the earth picks up their signals and sends them to us here on earth. You can read it for yourself, Mr. Kettelson. The information is in the W volume. I'll be glad to lend it to you."

Mr. Kettelson hung his head.

"I'm not much of a reader," he said.

"Oh?" Miss Pickerell exclaimed.

"What's more," Mr. Kettelson announced, while he walked through Miss Pickerell's parlor toward her front door, "I don't believe everything I read. And I don't think machines can ever take the place of people."

Miss Pickerell did not answer. She walked with Mr. Kettelson to the front door and waited for him to open it. She hoped he did not have anything more to say. His conversation was disturbing. She really did not trust machines either. She especially did not trust computers. The one in the Square Toe City department store had billed her $493.00 for a ball of yarn and a pair of knitting needles last month. Of course, it wasn't actually the computer that had made the mistake. It was the person who had programmed the computer. But if that person didn't have to work with a computer, he wouldn't be making such an error. And computers fitted in somewhere in the weather forecasting program. She didn't remember exactly where.

"Well, I'll be going now," Mr. Kettelson said, opening the door while Miss Pickerell breathed a sigh of relief. "Thank you very much for . . ."

An enormously loud rumbling noise interrupted whatever else he was going to say.

"Thunder!" Mr. Kettelson shouted. "Thunder, by golly!"

"My cow!" Miss Pickerell screamed. "I must get her back into the barn. I must go and . . ."

"I'll do it," Mr. Kettelson said, rushing out instantly. "I'll do it for you."

As Miss Pickerell watched him race off in the direction of the pastures, she felt her heart sink down into her shoes. She no longer knew what to think. Even in this age of modern technology, there were errors.

"Only I don't know just what kind of error this is or what is causing it," Miss Pickerell complained out loud. "And that makes it even worse."

She also felt worried about her seven nieces and nephews. She was just about to go inside and telephone their mother to learn which bus they had taken when she heard them calling from the farmyard gate. It was raining heavily now and they were running as fast as they could toward the house. For one terrible moment, they reminded her of the children climbing up the mountain on the day of the flood.

"But that's nonsense!" Miss Pickerell said, talking out loud again.

She stood up straight, took a firm hold on herself, and pushed the unwelcome thought out of her head.

2

An Unexpected Journey

Before Miss Pickerell could even tell her seven nieces and nephews to take their shoes off if they did not want to catch their death of cold, most of them had rushed into her bedroom. Miss Pickerell heard them arguing about which television program to listen to. They settled on one that seemed to Miss Pickerell to be all about teenagers, police, and gangsters. The voices of the actors came blaring into the kitchen where Euphus, her middle nephew, and Rosemary, her oldest niece, were sitting at the table. Pumpkins sat on the table in front of them.

11

"Why does it always have to rain on special days?" Euphus sighed. "I don't suppose you can take us to the observatory until it stops."

"No," said Miss Pickerell. "I can't."

"All Euphus can talk about is that giant laser at the observatory," said Rosemary. She began to stroke Pumpkins all the way from his head to the tip of his tail.

Pumpkins purred loudly. "May I pick you up, please?" Rosemary asked. Pumpkins purred louder.

"Thank you," Rosemary said, taking the big, black cat into her arms and giving him an affectionate pat on his head.

Miss Pickerell, mopping the floor where the children had tracked dirt in and putting sheets of newspaper down on the wet places, smiled her approval. Whatever else was wrong with Rosemary, she certainly knew how to behave with cats. She treated them with the respect and the dignity they deserved and they loved her for it.

"I think he wants to sit on my lap now," Euphus said, as he watched Rosemary scratch Pumpkins under the chin. "I can tell from the way he's looking at me."

"I'm sure he doesn't," Rosemary said, "but you can have him for a while."

She gently transferred Pumpkins to Euphus' arms. Then she headed for the long wardrobe mirror in Miss Pickerell's hall and began to comb her straight blond hair. It hung nearly to her shoulders now. For the thousandth time, Miss Pickerell wished that Rosemary would let her cut it.

Euphus got up to look at the sky. He wandered around the kitchen, then sat down at the table again.

"I imagine your cow is disappointed about not being able to take the trip to the observatory," he commented after a while.

Miss Pickerell said that she supposed she was. Miss Pickerell always took her animals with her when she went out in her automobile. The cow rode in a little red trailer that was attached to the automobile. The trailer had a canvas awning over it to protect the cow against bad weather. Pumpkins sat in the front seat next to Miss Pickerell. He was an excellent traveler.

"The cow's not half as disappointed as Euphus," Rosemary said, as she squinted at herself in the mirror, told Miss Pickerell that it was about time she bought herself a new mirror, and came back into the kitchen. "He hasn't talked about anything but the laser for a week."

Euphus immediately began to tell Miss Pickerell that the laser was a very important discovery, that it was a machine able to produce a light wave intense enough to penetrate steel and even explode rockets, that the giant laser at the astronomical observatory had bounced a light beam off the moon, that it took the beam about two and a half seconds to go there and come back, that the beam could be used to communicate with intelligent beings, if there were any, on planets of other stars, that . . .

Miss Pickerell stopped listening. She wasn't particularly interested in laser beams. The shouts and bullet sounds coming from the television set were giving her a headache. And she was still worried about the mistaken weather forecast.

"Euphus," she asked, "do you know how the weather computers work?"

"Of course I know," Euphus replied instantly. "I studied it in my science class. Do you want me to tell you about it?"

"Please," Miss Pickerell said.

"Well," Euphus said, "they really work the way any other computers work. There are computers on earth and computers on the space station. The computers on the space station get the information from the satellites and relay it to the computers on earth. It's simple."

"But," Miss Pickerell persisted, "suppose the computers make an error, suppose they . . ."

"They can't," Euphus said immediately. "The men on the space station keep a constant check on them."

Miss Pickerell thought again of her $493.00 bill for the ball of yarn and the two knitting needles. She wondered who kept a check on the department store computers. She looked at Euphus and nearly said, "Pooh!"

"If you like," Euphus went on, "I can tell you in detail about how the space station orbits and how it meets the weather satellites at certain times to make the checkups. I can also explain about those."

"Not now," Miss Pickerell replied, a little impatiently. She was feeling even more anxious than before. All sorts of frightening ideas about what might happen were coming into her head. She could hardly bear to think about them.

"Maybe if I write them down, they will all seem very silly," she told herself hopefully.

She walked over to the pantry where she kept her stationery supplies. She took a pad of paper and a thick yellow pencil down from a shelf. She sharpened the pencil with a kitchen knife before she sat down.

"I think I'd better print," she said. "My thumb won't hurt quite so much if I can hold the pencil more loosely and make big letters.''

The children said nothing. They moved their chairs as close to hers as they could and read to themselves what she was printing:

1. Square Toe County now has a reservoir that stores up rain water, and it also has a dam.

2. When the water in the reservoir gets too high, a gate in the dam is opened and the water flows out slowly and safely.

3. The extra water runs through the gate in the dam into Square Toe River.

4. But, *but,* I repeat, the gate is opened only when the weather satellites predict a heavy rain. Otherwise we would be wasting precious water that might be needed in a dry spell.

5. And the weather satellites have not predicted a heavy rain. They have predicted no rain at all. The weather forecast is for clear sunny skies.

6. What will happen if it keeps on raining and the weather satellites keep on predicting fair weather??? Mercy, what will . . .

"You don't have to worry about that any more," Euphus' voice suddenly said in her ear.

Miss Pickerell was so startled, she nearly jumped out of her chair.

She looked up to see Euphus and Rosemary smiling happily.

"It's stopped raining," Rosemary said.

"The sun is shining," Euphus announced.

In less than a minute, all of her seven nieces and nephews were surrounding her and clamoring to be taken to the observatory. Miss Pickerell was so relieved, she didn't even mind the noise they were making.

"I'll just go get my cow," she said.

She walked briskly down the three wooden steps outside her kitchen door, across the lawn where the hydrangeas were in full bloom, and through the lower pasture to the barn. Mr. Kettelson was standing in front of the barn door. Even he was smiling.

"Your cow's fine, Miss Pickerell," he said. "She was a little nervous with all that thunder. But I assured her that it would stop soon."

"And it has," Miss Pickerell said cheerfully. "The weather forecast was right, after all."

"Well, I wouldn't go as far as that," Mr. Kettelson answered, more cautiously. "It made no mention of a thunderstorm."

"Maybe a brief summer shower doesn't count in satellite weather forecasting," Miss Pickerell laughed.

"Maybe," Mr. Kettelson said, sounding rather doubtful.

"My seven nieces and nephews are here," Miss Pickerell said, noticing the uncertainty in his voice but deciding to ignore it. "We're all going to the astronomical observatory now."

"Your cow, too?" Mr. Kettelson asked.

"Naturally," Miss Pickerell told him.

Mr. Kettelson sighed but he helped Miss Pickerell lead the cow up the ramp and into her trailer and stayed in the trailer with her while Miss Pickerell drove around to the front of her house. The children and Pumpkins were already waiting there. Euphus handed Miss Pickerell her black straw hat and her big black umbrella. Miss Pickerell never went anywhere without her hat and her umbrella. She looked in the rear-view

19

mirror to make sure she was putting the hat on straight, asked Dwight, her oldest nephew, to turn his transistor radio off, and waited for all the children to crowd into the car. Rosemary sat in front, next to Miss Pickerell, with Pumpkins on her lap. Mr. Kettelson waved energetically when they finally drove away.

The private road that led from Miss Pickerell's farm down into the valley and on to the main highway was muddy from the rain. Miss Pickerell had to be very careful about not getting stuck in the mud. She also had to concentrate on her driving as she steered the car slowly around the descending mountain curves. If she had not been concentrating so hard, she might have noticed that the sun was disappearing again and that huge black clouds were ominously gathering over the mountains on the other side of the valley.

3

Mr. Esticott Says "No!"

The instant she saw the rapidly growing
dark patches of sky ahead, Miss Pickerell
turned the car around. It was not a minute
too soon. The rain followed her all the way
back to the farm.

She drove first to the barn where she put
the cow in her stall and made certain that
the barn door was closed and the shade
drawn down over the high window. She did
not want the cow to be frightened by any
possible flashes of lightning she might see
in the sky. Then Miss Pickerell drove the
children up to the house. They were all

shouting at once, arguing about the reasons for such unexpected weather behavior.

Miss Pickerell did not go into the house. She handed Pumpkins over to Rosemary. She asked Rosemary to be sure that all the children had some lunch. Miss Pickerell also borrowed Dwight's transistor radio. She didn't answer the children's questions about where she was going.

"I'll be back soon," she called, as she drove the car down her muddy private road once more. It was raining hard now. And the winds were high. Miss Pickerell's heart beat wildly when it seemed to her that the automobile was shaking from side to side.

"I must really be imagining things this time," she told herself sternly. "It can't be happening."

But she was almost positive that the wind was pushing the old automobile off its four wheels when she drove around a particularly sharp mountain curve. There was, at this point, only a sheer drop of about 3,000 feet between her and the valley below. Miss Pickerell stopped. She simply could not go on.

The weather forecast on Dwight's transistor radio was still for clear, sunny

weather. Miss Pickerell could hardly believe her ears as she listened to it and
heard, at the same time, the ceaseless beat-
ing of the heavy rain on the roof of the car
and on its windows. She kept getting angrier and angrier about the weather forecast. She got so angry, finally, she began
to drive again without thinking.

At the turn-off point that led to the main
highway, she remembered her fears, however. She tried to tell herself that she didn't
have anything to worry about with her automobile.

"They don't make cars the way they
made this one any more," she said vigorously. "The new ones aren't half as good.
People buy them for their looks, which is
ridiculous."

The man inside the filling station where
the highway began motioned through his
window for her to turn back. Miss Pickerell shouted that she was just going to the
reservoir which was only half a mile away.
Miss Pickerell didn't think the man heard
her over the noise that the wind was making. She believed it was only polite of her
to try to answer him, though.

She had to keep peering through the

windshield to find the narrow country road that led from the highway to the reservoir. And when she was finally on the road, she had to watch out for the very muddy places. She could hardly see them through her glasses, which were all clouded up, or through the windshield that was dry only for the second when the wipers moved across it. But she could distinctly feel the car sloshing around in mud most of the time.

"If I get stuck," she said, talking out loud in a desperate voice, "I won't be able to do anything about the flood. And I'm practically sure that there's going to be one."

Once, she was very nearly stuck and she told herself bitterly that she should have called the Governor and alerted him to the dangers instead of making this terrible trip by herself.

"But he never would have agreed with me," she reasoned. "So what would have been the use? I had to come. I simply had to!"

The reservoir was located in a tree-clustered area that Miss Pickerell knew very well. She often stopped by there, when she was returning from a trip to the crowded Square Toe City supermarket, to listen to the birds and to enjoy the peaceful scene. Now, she enjoyed only the fact that she was moving, inch by inch, closer to the little log cabin that Covington, the young man in charge of the reservoir, used as his headquarters. Miss Pickerell liked Covington. He had stopped being an animal trainer and was now studying to become a veterinarian. That's why he took the job at the reservoir. It gave him time to study. Miss Pickerell reflected, as she got out of her automobile and tried to open her umbrella, that Covington would understand about the mistaken weather forecast and would open the gate in the dam immediately to prevent another flood.

It was not Covington, however, who answered the door in response to her knock, pulled her inside, and helped her into one of the two straight-backed chairs in the cabin. It was Mr. Esticott, the train conductor, wearing his conductor's uniform with the gold buttons down the front and the vest that didn't quite meet across his stomach.

"Mr. Esticott?" Miss Pickerell exclaimed, staring. "What are you doing here?"

"I'm the summer replacement," Mr. Esticott replied, as he sat down in the other chair. "Covington's on vacation."

"But . . . but . . . ," Miss Pickerell spluttered, looking at Mr. Esticott's uniform again. "What about your own job? Have you been discharged?"

"Oh, no!" Mr. Esticott laughed. "This is my vacation, too. I was planning to go visit my daughter in Plentibush City. But Covington couldn't go on vacation if he didn't get someone to replace him. So I volunteered. I don't mind. Of course, his reservoir attendant uniform doesn't fit me. And it doesn't pay to make one up special for me. That's why . . ."

"When will Covington be back?" Miss Pickerell asked.

"Oh, he has only ten days," Mr. Esticott replied. "And he left on Saturday. Today's Monday. That means he'll be back on . . ."

Miss Pickerell thought hard while Mr. Esticott counted off the days on his fingers. It would take longer to explain things to Mr. Esticott than to Covington. But she had to do it. She decided to come directly to the point.

"Mr. Esticott," she said.

"Yes, Miss Pickerell?" Mr. Esticott replied, his fingers still in mid-air.

"Mr. Esticott," Miss Pickerell went on, "do you know about the gate in the dam?"

"Of course I know about the gate in the dam," Mr. Esticott said stiffly. "How could I take on Covington's job if I didn't know about the gate in the dam?"

"Well," Miss Pickerell said, "we must open that gate immediately."

Mr. Esticott looked shocked.

"Miss Pickerell," he said, "it may be that you don't know the special conditions under which that gate may be opened."

"I know the conditions," Miss Pickerell replied. "The gate to the dam is opened when the water in the reservoir gets too high."

"Not exactly," Mr. Esticott said, sounding very official. "The gate is opened when the weather forecast is for a heavy rain."

He walked over to the large radio that stood against the wall.

"Don't bother to turn it on, Mr. Esticott," Miss Pickerell said, impatiently. "I've just listened to the forecast on my oldest nephew's transistor set."

"I wasn't going to turn it on," Mr. Esticott said, with offended dignity. "I was going to point out to you, Miss Pickerell, the button that is in the middle of this radio. It turns a bright red when the forecast is for rain. That's the signal for me to open the gate. I don't have to listen to the weather report."

Miss Pickerell could only feel a sense of absolute horror. It was pouring buckets outside the little cabin. Some of the rain was even splashing in through the spaces, here and there, between the logs and making large puddles of water on the floor. And Mr. Esticott was sitting calmly and talking about waiting for a signal. She wondered if she would be able to reason with him.

"Mr. Esticott," she asked, "do you remember the flood we once had in Square Toe County?"

Mr. Esticott objected with, for him, surprising speed. He talked about the weather satellites. He sounded, Miss Pickerell thought, exactly the way she had this morning when she was talking to Mr. Kettelson, the hardware store man. Miss Pickerell sighed. It seemed entirely possible that Mr. Kettelson and she were the only people in Square Toe County who didn't have complete faith in machines.

"Mr. Esticott," she asked hopelessly, "has it ever occurred to you that the weather satellites might be wrong?"

"That . . . that may be," Mr. Esticott said, slowly.

"Well, then . . . ," Miss Pickerell said, standing up.

"But I have my orders," Mr. Esticott said, standing up, too. "I was told never, absolutely never, to open the gate until that light turned red."

"Do you mean," Miss Pickerell asked, finding it almost impossible to believe what she heard, "that you don't have the responsibility of looking out of the window and making a decision for yourself?"

Mr. Esticott coughed. He looked very embarrassed.

"No," he said, lowering his eyes. "They never gave me that responsibility."

Miss Pickerell had nothing to say. She believed in obeying orders, too. She stared at the button in the middle of the radio. It gave no sign of turning red. And the puddles of water on the floor were growing into pools. There had to be something she could do.

"Mr. Esticott," she asked, "do you have a telephone?"

"Yes," Mr. Esticott replied. "On the table in the back. But it's for official business only."

"This is very official business," Miss Pickerell said, jumping over two pools of water and wading across a third as she made her way to the back. "I'm calling the Governor."

4

Miss Pickerell Hopes
for the Best

Mr. Esticott's telephone was not working.
Miss Pickerell did not realize this at first.
She dialed the Governor's number the
minute she picked up the receiver. She
heard no ringing at the other end of the
connection.

She felt very exasperated when it occurred to her that she had forgotten to wait
for the dial tone.

"Every second counts now," she cautioned herself. "I must be more careful."

She gave her full attention to listening
for the dial sound when she tried calling
again. There was none. No one answered

when she dialed the operator, either. Miss Pickerell tried screaming "Operator" into the mouthpiece, too. Nothing happened. The telephone had definitely gone dead.

"This is the last straw!" Miss Pickerell exclaimed. "Positively the last straw!"

She was just about to go over and discuss the problem with Mr. Esticott when she remembered the public telephone booth across the road. She recalled it distinctly because she had used that telephone once when she left a pair of practically new gloves on the supermarket check-out counter. The cashier there had been very polite and helpful. He told her that he had her gloves. He would be sure to keep them for her in a safe place until she came for them. Miss Pickerell had been very grateful.

"I'll call the Governor from the same place now," she told herself, comfortingly. "And while I'm at it, I'll call Emergency Repairs to tell them that Mr. Esticott's telephone is out of order."

She hunted rapidly in the telephone directory for the Emergency Repairs number. It was on page one, printed very large. Miss Pickerell copied it on the back of the laundry list that she found in her handbag. She also copied down Mr. Esticott's number so that she could give it to Emergency Repairs. She looked around for Mr. Esticott to tell him where she was going. He did not seem to be in the cabin any more. Miss Pickerell saw him standing at the edge of the reservoir when she ran across the road. She did not want to stop then.

The public telephone was in perfect working order. Miss Pickerell breathed a sigh of relief as she dialed the Governor's number. The line was busy.

She called Emergency Repairs while she waited for the Governor to get off the line. A man answered. Miss Pickerell gave him Mr. Esticott's number, told him exactly what was wrong, and talked to him about how important it was that something be done right away.

"You see," she explained carefully, "the Governor will undoubtedly want to speak to Mr. Esticott about this terrible situation."

"The telephone will be repaired within the next twenty-four hours," the man replied coolly.

"Twenty-four hours!" Miss Pickerell

34

gasped. She was so shocked, she nearly choked getting the words out. "But I told you. This is a very critical emergency. It may easily become a matter of life and death."

"Thank you for calling," the man said.

He went off the line.

Miss Pickerell tried to keep calm. She told herself that the days when telephone operators always had time to listen to their customers and even, sometimes, to make sympathetic suggestions were gone forever. She had to remember that. But she still felt absolutely furious with the Emergency Repairs man. Why, he didn't even *care* about the emergency. He . . . he acted almost exactly like a machine, himself.

The Governor's line was still busy. Miss Pickerell wondered whether his wife was on the wire. Many calls came into the Governor's office. Miss Pickerell knew that. She felt certain, however, that no one talked as long on those calls as the Governor's wife.

Miss Pickerell debated with herself about sending the Governor a telegram. She decided that it was a very good idea. She could include something in the telegram about the inconsiderate behavior of the Square Toe County Emergency Repairs Service. The prospect made her feel much better. She asked the operator to connect her with the telegraph office.

She waited as patiently as she could while she listened to the rings in the telegraph office. She knew just what was happening. When the telegraph people were busy on one telephone, they simply let the others keep on ringing. That could go on forever.

Miss Pickerell gave up. She suddenly felt very tired. She walked slowly across the road to the reservoir headquarters. It was raining very little now. But the skies overhead were dark. And her thumb was more painful than ever.

Mr. Esticott was sitting in his chair when she entered the cabin. His face was ashen white.

"We're in trouble, Miss Pickerell," he said, the minute he saw her.

"If you mean that your telephone is not working," Miss Pickerell replied, "I've just called the Emergency Repairs Service."

"We're in more trouble than that, Miss Pickerell," Mr. Esticott went on.

Miss Pickerell sat down. She waited for Mr. Esticott to go on. He said "Miss Pickerell" several times, but then he stopped. He couldn't seem to continue. He got up now and walked over to the window.

"Miss Pickerell," he said, without looking at her, "I was very much upset by what you said about the possibility of a flood. I went out to observe the reservoir."

"Yes," Miss Pickerell replied. "I noticed that."

"The water, Miss Pickerell," Mr. Esticott said, suddenly turning around and talking very fast, "the water in the reservoir is only two inches from the top. Do you know what that means?"

Miss Pickerell knew only too well. If it began to rain again and the water rose another two inches, the reservoir would overflow. Then it would flow over the dam, come crashing into the town, and . . . She refused to think of what could happen.

"Did you speak to the Governor?" Mr. Esticott asked.

"His line was busy," Miss Pickerell said dully.

She stared at the button in the middle of the radio. Mr. Esticott stared, too.

"I hope you understand, Miss Pickerell," he said, uneasily, "that I really must wait for the signal before I can . . ."

"I understand perfectly," Miss Pickerell said, almost wishing that she didn't.

"What are we going to do?" Mr. Esticott pleaded.

Miss Pickerell got up.

"I don't know what you're going to do,

Mr. Esticott," she said firmly. "But I know what I *have* to do. I'm driving to the Governor's office."

"It's a two-hour drive," Mr. Esticott exclaimed. "At normal speed, that is. And you . . ."

Mr. Esticott stopped and looked away.

"And I never drive more than twenty-five miles an hour," Miss Pickerell finished for him. "That's what you were going to say, isn't it, Mr. Esticott?"

Mr. Esticott nodded unhappily.

"I've been known to drive at thirty," Miss Pickerell said.

Mr. Esticott did not answer.

"I imagine," Miss Pickerell went on, "that, if necessary, I might go even faster than that."

"In the middle of a storm?" Mr. Esticott asked incredulously.

"It's not storming now," Miss Pickerell said, talking more to herself than to Mr. Esticott.

"That doesn't mean it won't start again in a minute," Mr. Esticott said.

Miss Pickerell had thought of that, too. She wished Mr. Esticott hadn't put it into words for her. She wasn't exactly looking forward to the drive to the Governor's office.

"I'll just have to hope for the best," she said, as she straightened her hat, made sure that she had her handbag and her umbrella, and walked resolutely out to her car.

5

Miss Pickerell Makes
Up Her Mind

It did not begin to rain hard again until
Miss Pickerell was on the main highway.
Then the thunder roared, the lightning
flashed, and the rain poured steadily from
the dark skies. Miss Pickerell was sure that
it was raining in the state capital, as well
as in Square Toe County. The Governor
would need little convincing about the need
to open the gate in the dam. She could only
hope that he would give the order before
the reservoir began to overflow.

"Maybe his telephone is free now," she
thought. "I'd feel so much better if I could
talk to him."

She decided to stop at the Square Toe County Weather Station to try to call again. Her friend, Mr. Humwhistel, was in charge of the earth computers at the weather station. Miss Pickerell positively shivered as she thought about this. Computers handled by most people were probably risky enough. But computers controlled by anyone as absent-minded as Mr. Humwhistel . . . Miss Pickerell preferred not even to think about it.

The weather station was on the main road. Miss Pickerell recognized the building by the large green dome on its roof and by the tower that pointed straight up from the dome. She remembered that there were antennae all around the tower. She remembered, too, what Mr. Humwhistel had once told her about communicating with his weather colleagues on the space station.

"The picture part works like television," Mr. Humwhistel said then. "I just turn the knob. And we talk to each other over a radio-telephone system."

Mr. Humwhistel had been a very fine teacher when he worked in the Square Toe City High School, Miss Pickerell reflected, as she walked up to the heavy bronze door that led into the weather station. Personally, she wished he would go back to teaching and leave the computers alone.

A guard in a gray uniform, standing under an umbrella almost as big as her own, told Miss Pickerell that absolutely no visitors were allowed.

"I'm not really visiting," Miss Pickerell said, not knowing exactly how to explain that all she actually wanted was to make a telephone call. It would sound entirely unreasonable if she said just that. And if she started to tell the whole story . . . She could hardly take the time to do that.

The guard was peering at her very suspiciously now.

"Yes?" he asked.

"I'm . . . I'm a friend of Mr. Humwhistel's," Miss Pickerell said quickly.

"Oh!" the guard replied.

To Miss Pickerell's surprise, he seemed greatly impressed. He closed her umbrella for her, sheltered her under his own while he escorted her inside, and advised her to talk to a young woman sitting at a white desk in the middle of a lobby.

"My umbrella?" Miss Pickerell asked anxiously.

"It will be waiting for you in this umbrella stand," the guard replied, putting the umbrella there. "The young woman will keep an eye on it."

The young woman, who wore her dark brown hair down to her waist and had large purple-tinted spectacles on, didn't strike Miss Pickerell as very responsible.

"I'm probably prejudiced," Miss Pickerell reassured herself. "That's the style, these days. It doesn't have to mean that she's not a good worker."

In any case, Miss Pickerell didn't know what else to do with her umbrella. She certainly didn't want to carry it along and ruin the highly polished floor she was walking on.

"I'm here to see Mr. Humwhistel," she said, when she got to the desk. "My name is Lavinia Pickerell."

"Spell the last name, please," the young woman said.

She wrote each letter down as Miss Pickerell gave it to her, then proceeded to spell it into an intercom speaker. Mr. Humwhistel was in the lobby before she reached the letter K.

"Good morning, Miss Pickerell," he said, smiling broadly. "Or is it afternoon by now? I suppose it's afternoon. I'm never sure. Please come in."

He put his arm under her elbow and steered her through a large room where six young men were very intently watching six absolutely blank television screens.

"Forevermore!" Miss Pickerell breathed, when she saw this. Mr. Humwhistel did not appear to notice. He opened the door to a small office, waited for her to go first, and helped her into a chair. He sat down behind a white desk exactly like the one in the lobby.

"Well, Miss Pickerell," he asked, while he hunted in both jacket pockets for his pipe. "What can I do for you today?"

Miss Pickerell came to the point at once.

"I would like to use your telephone," she said. "To make a very important call."

Mr. Humwhistel pushed back the gold-rimmed glasses that were resting on the edge of his nose, looked sharply at Miss Pickerell, and asked, "To the Governor? To talk to him about unlocking the gate in the dam?"

45

It was Miss Pickerell's turn to stare.

"How . . . how did you know?" she spluttered.

Mr. Humwhistel laughed.

"I was sure you would think of that, Miss Pickerell," he said.

"I tried calling from the reservoir," Miss Pickerell went on. "I couldn't . . ."

"It doesn't matter," Mr. Humwhistel told her. "I've already spoken to the Governor."

Miss Pickerell stood up.

"I can't begin to tell you how relieved I am," she said to Mr. Humwhistel. "I'll go home now. I left my seven nieces and nephews in the house with Pumpkins and the cow and . . . ."

"I think you'd better sit down again, Miss Pickerell," Mr. Humwhistel said, not letting her finish. "I have something else to tell you."

Miss Pickerell sat down. Mr. Humwhistel puffed on his pipe. He didn't seem to know that it was not lit.

"Miss Pickerell," he said, between puffs, "the Governor is not going to do anything about having the gate in the dam opened right now."

"What!" Miss Pickerell shouted.

"The Governor says it is no longer raining in the state capital," Mr. Humwhistel went on, still puffing. "He feels reasonably certain that it will stop raining here soon, too."

"Reasonably certain!" Miss Pickerell said, trying hard not to scream.

"Well, let us say he hopes so, Miss Pickerell," Mr. Humwhistel continued. "He has to consult with a number of people and agencies before he can give any order about the dam. You understand, we have never had this kind of weather complication before. And he has other things to worry about right now."

"That's perfectly ridiculous!" Miss Pickerell replied. "The Governor couldn't have said any such thing. What are you talking about, Mr. Humwhistel?"

Mr. Humwhistel seemed to hesitate. He searched on his desk for his matches and relit his pipe before he answered.

"I don't like to alarm you, Miss Pickerell," he said, at last, "but you probably realize that something has gone wrong with our weather forecasting process."

Miss Pickerell assured Mr. Humwhistel that she certainly did realize it.

"But," she went on, "you can get in touch with the space station and find out what is wrong. You told me yourself how easy it was. You said that . . ."

"Miss Pickerell," Mr. Humwhistel interrupted, "did you, by any chance, notice what the young men in my outer office were doing?"

"Staring at blank television screens," Miss Pickerell answered indignantly.

"That's just it," Mr. Humwhistel said, sighing so deeply that the top button on his jacket snapped off. "Our communications system has broken down, too. We can't establish any contact whatsoever with the space station."

He stooped to pick up his jacket button, then began pacing the floor.

"The President may call a conference of Governors and of outstanding space experts," he said.

"That can go on for days," Miss Pickerell muttered under her breath. "And then, they'll probably appoint a committee."

Mr. Humwhistel stopped in the middle of his pacing.

"I'm sorry," he said. "I didn't hear you, Miss Pickerell. What did you say?"

"Nothing," Miss Pickerell replied.

She was doing some very fast thinking. She was coming to a very simple conclusion, too. But she wanted a few questions answered before she took any action.

"Mr. Humwhistel," she asked, "do you think it will stop raining?"

"I don't know," Mr. Humwhistel said, looking out of the window. "It seems to be letting up now."

"It did that before, too," Miss Pickerell said. "Do you think it will let up for good this time?"

Mr. Humwhistel shrugged his shoulders. Miss Pickerell thought of the pain in her thumb and believed she could answer that question better than he could.

"Let me ask you something else, Mr. Humwhistel," she said.

"Please do," Mr. Humwhistel answered, sitting down.

"If the weather satellite began to give a definite forecast of continued rain," she asked, "would the Governor see to it that the gate to the dam was opened?"

"Naturally," Mr. Humwhistel said, instantly. "But he wouldn't even have to give his permission, if that happened. The gate is always opened when the weather satellite predicts . . ."

"Well then," Miss Pickerell interrupted, as she got up from her chair, "there seems to be only one thing to do."

"What's that?" Mr. Humwhistel asked immediately.

"Someone has to go up to the space station, fix whatever is wrong, and get that weather satellite to forecast some accurate information," Miss Pickerell said.

"Just whom do you have in mind?" Mr. Humwhistel asked, looking at her very oddly.

Miss Pickerell did not answer the question right away. She was thinking about Pumpkins and her cow and of how much she wanted to be with them this very minute. She was wondering, too, why strange things always seemed to happen to her. She had talked to Mr. Kettelson about that this morning, she remembered.

"Mr. Humwhistel," she asked, when she forced herself to stop dwelling on these thoughts, "is Deputy Administrator

Blakely still in charge of shuttle flights to outer space?''

"I . . . I believe so," Mr. Humwhistel said.

"That's all right then," Miss Pickerell said. "I'm almost certain that I can convince him."

"Convince him to do what?" Mr. Humwhistel asked, the suspicion quickly growing in his eyes.

"To put me on the next shuttle to the space station," Miss Pickerell answered. "I have just made up my mind to do something to keep another disastrous flood from engulfing Square Toe County."

She marched quickly out of Mr. Humwhistel's office. She noticed, as she went, that Mr. Humwhistel's mouth was wide open and that his pipe had fallen out of his mouth and onto one of his knees. She hoped he would remember to pick the pipe up before the hot ash burned a hole in his pants.

6

A Ticket to Outer Space

It seemed to Miss Pickerell that Deputy Administrator Horace T. Blakely shuddered a little when his assistant ushered her into his private office. Apart from that, he looked to her exactly the same. His hair was gray and parted neatly in the middle and his posture was just as rigidly correct as the last time she saw him. Even his office had not changed. The bulging briefcase stood at the side of his desk. And his walls were still covered with charts and astronomical maps and routes of space flights.

Miss Pickerell knew, of course, why he was not too glad to see her. She had practically forced him to let her get on the cargo

ship that took her to the moon. If necessary, she had every intention of doing the
same thing to get on the shuttle to the space
station.

"Good afternoon, Miss Pickerell," he
said. "It is nice to see that you are in good
health. May I say, without wasting any
time, that I assume you have a mission that
has brought you here today?"

"I have, indeed," Miss Pickerell replied, trying to be as curt as the deputy
administrator.

"May I know what it is?" Mr. Blakely
asked.

"Certainly, Deputy Administrator
Blakely," Miss Pickerell said. "I must get
to the space station as quickly as possible.
I have to do something about the weather
satellites. It is very important."

The deputy administrator knew better
than to contradict her. But he frowned.

"Please call me Mr. Blakely," he reminded her. "I've talked to you about that
in the past."

"Oh, yes," Miss Pickerell said apologetically. "I keep forgetting."

"I thought so," Mr. Blakely commented.

He got up to examine one of the charts on the wall.

"We have two shuttle flights to the space station this week," he said. "The first one leaves from the Square Toe space field in an hour. The second goes on Thursday."

"I'll go today," Miss Pickerell said.

The deputy administrator arched his eyebrows.

"But you have no permission to make this flight," he said.

"Permission!" Miss Pickerell exclaimed. "For a shuttle flight?"

"For a shuttle flight into space, Miss Pickerell," Mr. Blakely corrected her. "We are planning, in the not-too-distant future, perhaps, to make these flights available to the general public. There will probably be tourist parties and guided tours. I am not at all in favor of that sort of plan. I don't like crowds. And besides . . ."

"From whom," Miss Pickerell asked, returning to the point, "do people who want to go on shuttle flights get their permission?"

"Well, there are various rules," Mr. Blakely said, walking back to his desk for a thick book of regulations which he began to thumb through. "Minors—people under the legal age, that is—have to get permission from their parents."

He looked apologetically at Miss Pickerell.

"I know that doesn't apply to you," he said.

"Certainly not," Miss Pickerell replied.

Mr. Blakely turned pages.

"Then there is the regulation," he went on, "about people who want to conduct experiments in outer space. They have to get permission from the government. But I don't suppose that regulation applies to you, either, Miss Pickerell. When you spoke of doing something about the weather satellite, you didn't have an experiment in mind, did you?"

"No," Miss Pickerell said, "I wouldn't dream of such a thing."

"There is also the regulation about . . . ," the deputy administrator went on, turning more pages.

"Mr. Blakely," Miss Pickerell interrupted, feeling absolutely desperate, "please believe me when I tell you that it is most important for me to get up to the space station. And I can't . . . I really

can't lose any more time. You said the next shuttle was leaving in an hour."

"In less than an hour now," came a booming voice from the doorway. "And she's right. We haven't a moment to lose."

Miss Pickerell and the deputy administrator both turned around. It was the Governor, dressed, as usual, in his fine, double-breasted dark suit, his shining, black top hat, and his immaculate white gloves. Miss Pickerell gasped.

"I've arranged to have a limousine take us to the launch pad. What's more," the Governor went on, "I'm going up to the space station with her. You may charge Miss Pickerell's ticket to the State, Mr. Blakely. I imagine you have a seat for me next to her."

"It . . . it can be arranged, Governor," the deputy administrator said weakly.

"How . . . how did you know where to . . . ," Miss Pickerell began.

"Mr. Humwhistel told me," the Governor said, immediately. "Naturally, I told him that I wouldn't think of letting Miss Pickerell make such a trip alone. The state of the weather in Square Toe County is my official responsibility."

Miss Pickerell thought that the Governor was getting it all mixed up. He meant that the state of the gate in the dam was his responsibility. But she didn't say anything.

"I also advised the President," the Governor continued, "that I believed it was more essential for me to take a look at the weather satellite than to attend a meeting right now. We still haven't re-established communications with outer space."

He sighed heavily.

Miss Pickerell did not dare to question the Governor's actions. But she felt that she simply *had* to bring up the matter of the dam.

"If . . . if," she asked, nearly stuttering, "if you're not there, Governor, who will give the order about opening the gate in the dam?"

"We don't have to worry about that," the Governor said, cheerily. "It isn't raining any more."

Miss Pickerell wanted to tell him that it would rain again, but Mr. Blakely's assistant poked his head in through the door at that very moment. The deputy administrator spoke quickly to Miss Pickerell and to the Governor.

"The transport to the launch pad is here," he said. "You'll have to hurry. The space suits are on the shuttle. The stewardess will help you on with them before take-off."

"Thank you," Miss Pickerell and the Governor both said, a little breathlessly. The Governor also said that he hoped the space suit would fit over his top hat.

"I keep forgetting it when I take it off," he explained. "I can't begin to tell you how many I lose every month."

Miss Pickerell knew just what he meant. She had exactly the same kind of trouble with umbrellas. Only a little while ago she had nearly left hers in the stand at the Weather Station. She held on to her big, black umbrella very firmly now as she stood up.

"Let's go," the Governor said.

"I must make two phone calls," Miss Pickerell said.

"It's twenty minutes to lift-off," the assistant cautioned.

Miss Pickerell nodded.

She called her house first. Rosemary answered. Miss Pickerell explained that she was leaving for the space station and that she would be back as soon as she could. She did not give Rosemary a chance to interrupt. She gave full instructions about the care of Pumpkins and the cow and said that she was calling Rosemary's parents next to ask if they would stay on the farm.

"That really isn't necessary," Rosemary objected. "I know how to manage. And I can get Mr. Kettelson to come in and talk to the cow, if you'd like that."

Miss Pickerell's brother and his wife said that they understood, when she called them, and would leave for her farm immediately. They couldn't imagine why Miss Pickerell was taking the shuttle to the space station, however. They didn't approve of the idea, either. Space travel might be in an advanced stage, these days, but it still had its dangers. Miss Pickerell replied that she didn't have time to discuss this with them, said good-bye, and hung up.

The Governor courteously extended his arm to her.

"Shall we go, Miss Pickerell?" he asked.

60

"Yes," Miss Pickerell replied, talking very loud because she suddenly felt a jolt of nervous apprehension in her stomach. She told herself sternly that this was ridiculous. It wasn't as though she hadn't been up in outer space before. And space flights had become ordinary, well *almost* ordinary events. *Certainly,* they were far safer nowadays than traveling on a crowded highway. But it was no use. She couldn't help feeling frightened. She was very grateful that she had the Governor's strong arm to lean on.

7

Destination:
Space Station

But the Governor was nervous, too. Miss
Pickerell could tell by the way he kept on
smoothing his moustache when they were
in the limousine. And he did not even look
around when they reached the space field.
Not that there was much to see. Miss Pickerell and the Governor were ushered from
the car to a covered passageway that led
directly to the shuttle. Miss Pickerell had
only a moment to notice that the shuttle
was really two aircraft. The larger craft
looked like an ordinary jet, except that its
nose pointed straight up into the sky, and
there was a smaller aircraft attached to its

underbelly. She pointed this out to the Governor. He did not answer. He concentrated on escorting her up the ladder.

The young stewardess who helped Miss Pickerell on with her space suit was very sympathetic when Miss Pickerell told her about her fear of ladders.

"I thought I had gotten over it," Miss Pickerell explained, "until I fell off my barnyard ladder last year. Now, I just have to look at one to feel dizzy."

"There are some things people never get over," the stewardess said, shrugging her shoulders philosophically. "Personally, I have never gotten over the shock of the first few minutes of space travel. You know, the time when the shuttle separates from the booster vehicle. It's just as bad for me now as the first time."

"Oh!" said Miss Pickerell, wishing she hadn't brought up the subject. She followed the stewardess to a contour seat on the aisle and didn't say a word when the stewardess strapped her in. The Governor was already in the seat beside her. He looked very strange with the space helmet jammed on over his flattened top hat. He looked sick, too. Miss Pickerell couldn't make up her mind whether the color of his face was ash gray or pale green.

"It's only the take-off that's hard," she told him, as reassuringly as she could. "After that, we don't feel a thing."

The Governor muttered something. Miss Pickerell couldn't hear him, for the rocket engines had begun to roar. Almost immediately, a tremendous force pushed against her back, while another force drove her down into her chair, down, down, until all the breath was nearly out of her body and she thought that she and her chair were going to be crushed to smithereens. The spaceships slowly rose off the ground and thundered out into space. Miss Pickerell breathed easily again.

"We're off," the stewardess said, floating down the aisle and explaining that floating was natural when there was no gravity. Then, she floated back while she announced that passengers could take their space suits off now, if they wanted to.

"No space suits are necessary," she kept repeating. "This spacecraft has been filled with air at reduced pressure for our safety and comfort."

Miss Pickerell climbed out of her space

suit. The Governor just unzipped his space helmet and took off his top hat. He put the hat on an overhead rack. It floated off immediately. The stewardess rescued it at the other end of the cabin. She brought it back and tied it down securely on the rack.

"Please don't let me forget to take the hat with me," the Governor said anxiously to Miss Pickerell.

"I won't," Miss Pickerell promised.

"Maybe I ought to take a nap," the Governor said, leaning back in his chair and tightening all his straps. "I want to be very alert when we get to the space station."

Miss Pickerell agreed that this might be a good idea. She, herself, did not feel the least bit sleepy. She looked around at her fellow passengers. She counted ten men and a woman with a sleeping baby on her lap. Miss Pickerell thought the woman might be going up to the space station to visit her husband. He could be working there as an engineer or an astronomer or a weather expert or practically anything.

One man in the cabin reminded her of her old friend Mr. Rugby who ran the Square Toe County Diner. He was bald and just as stout. She tried to imagine why he was traveling up to the space station.

Speculating about the other passengers made Miss Pickerell feel drowsy. It was a little like daydreaming, she decided, pleasant and restful.

She leaned back in her chair and was just about to close her eyes when a voice came blaring over the loudspeaker. "Good afternoon," a man said. "This is Captain Kindle, speaking to you from the cockpit of the orbital ship Remus. In exactly thirty-two seconds we will execute the staging maneuver of our Tandem Space Shuttle. There will be a short thrust after we have disengaged from the booster ship as our own engines ignite."

The thrust woke up the Governor. He looked out the window and turned white. *"Look!"* he shouted. Miss Pickerell leaned across him and looked. There, falling back to earth, was the large booster.

"It's all right," said Miss Pickerell. "The captain explained about it while you were asleep."

"I wish he'd keep his mind on piloting," **the Governor** complained. "I thought we'd split in two!"

66

"We did," replied Miss Pickerell.

"Captain Kindle again," came the loudspeaker. "We are now in orbit and are cruising at a speed of 17,500 miles per hour. The orbit we are in will join the orbit of the space station approximately thirty-two minutes from now. And at that time we will perform a maneuver which will put us into a docking position close to the space station."

The spaceship rolled suddenly. The Governor stiffened.

"Out the windows on your left is one of the most beautiful sights you'll ever see," said Captain Kindle.

"Outrageous!" exploded the Governor. "This isn't a sightseeing mission. There's no time to waste!"

Miss Pickerell floated up to a window and craned her neck. The earth was right there in the middle of a vast expanse of darkness. It looked like the moon did from her farm on Square Toe Mountain except that it was brighter. Miss Pickerell clapped her hands in excitement.

"From where I sit," broke in the Captain again, "I can see valleys ringed around with mountains that are crowned in snow.

I can see blue-green oceans and rivers. But the most exciting thing for me is being able to see the earth, its size, its shape, everything about it from *outside* the earth—that is, from outer space."

Miss Pickerell couldn't agree more. Seeing the earth from outside was the best part. But she also liked the way the pilot had described the things he saw on earth. She wondered if he could remember it and write it down for her. She thought she'd like to show it to her seven nieces and nephews. She mentioned this to the Governor.

"Of course, he'll be able to write it down for you," the Governor scoffed. "He's probably got it all prepared for some news release or book he's authoring or, better still, for a television appearance on a talk show. He sounded like a publicity hound to me."

Miss Pickerell hadn't thought of this.

"I'm glad he's back at the controls now," the Governor added.

Miss Pickerell nodded absently. Then she sat bolt upright.

"Do you mean to say he's been away

from the controls?'' she asked, her mouth dropping open.

"Our pilot probably put the ship on automatic while he was talking to us," the Governor said, calmly. "Of course, we're perfectly safe because the space centers on earth keep a strict check and are in constant communication with . . ."

"Oh, no!" Miss Pickerell suddenly exclaimed, drawing in her breath in one long, shuddering gasp.

"What is it?" the Governor asked instantly.

"Nothing," Miss Pickerell said firmly. It had just occurred to her that if poor Mr. Humwhistel's TV screens were blank, communications between the space shuttle and the space centers might be cut off, too. She had no intention of sharing this terrible thought with the Governor, however.

"Why, without earth communication, that pilot's flying practically blind," she said to herself.

She made an effort to reassure herself by thinking of all the instruments a pilot could use to guide him. It wasn't very helpful.

"I've never heard of a space flight that

made it on instruments alone," she thought, miserably.

The Governor went back to his nap. Miss Pickerell sat, tightly strapped to her seat, listening for every sound the ship was making and feeling every movement. Once, she thought she heard what sounded like a soft explosion.

"That's impossible," she told herself sternly.

She also told herself that there was undoubtedly communication between the space station and the spaceship. She tried to figure out how near they might be to the space station. "We must be almost there," she thought. She leaned down to look at her watch.

And then the ship lurched.

"I *must* be imagining this," Miss Pickerell said out loud.

But she was not imagining. The lurching had awakened the Governor.

"What's happening?" he asked.

Miss Pickerell shook her head.

"What's happening?" the Governor called, looking back over his shoulder. "Stewardess! What's happening? Stewardess!" the Governor shouted, the color in his face turning purple. "I demand to know what is going on. Stewardess!"

The stewardess, using the hand grips to guide her, floated over to him. She looked very flustered.

"We've . . . we've docked," she said. "I've been trying to tell everybody. Ordinarily, we have a light on to announce it. But that doesn't seem to be working. And the captain didn't announce it over the loudspeaker because, I guess, he thought the light was on. I'd better go and talk to him."

"Just a minute, young lady," the Governor said firmly. "Please be so kind as to tell me where we are."

"Why, on the space station, of course," the stewardess said.

"Is that all there is to it?" Miss Pickerell asked in surprise.

"That's all there is to it," the stewardess explained. "Once the retro-rockets ignite and slow the ship down to the speed of the orbiting space station, the actual docking is a very quiet operation. The nose of our ship locks into a docking hole in the side of the space station."

"Oh," said Miss Pickerell. It was

certainly different from a boat docking.

The stewardess began to help Miss Pickerell on with her space suit.

"You don't really need to wear it," she commented. "The docking chamber is enclosed and pressurized. But I guess wearing this bulky thing is easier than carrying it."

Miss Pickerell agreed. She reminded the Governor to take his top hat and checked on her own umbrella and handbag.

"We're here," she said happily, as she took her place in the line of passengers waiting their turn to get off.

"Who knows what lies ahead for us?" the Governor replied.

He sounded grim. But he waved to the baby who was gurgling cheerfully in front of him and shook hands with the woman who was holding the child.

8

Sightseeing on the Space Station

"Forevermore!" Miss Pickerell breathed, as she floated through the docking chamber and into the lowest deck of the space station. She was in a cylindrical, stark-white room with stacks of floor-to-ceiling cartons of food and other supplies. In the center of this round room was another large tube. It had a door.

"This way," said the stewardess, pressing a button next to the door in the center tube. The passengers, including Miss Pickerell and the Governor, floated after her. "This is the elevator between decks. This space station has five decks—all five have

73

a zero 'g' environment. Some of the larger space stations have both zero and artificial gravity. Weightlessness is really very pleasant once you get used to it."

Miss Pickerell liked to keep her feet on the ground. It was impossible to do that here. The elevator door slid open. A red-headed, freckle-faced young man, wearing a gray, one-piece regulation coverall and a non-regulation baseball cap blocked the way. He held a clipboard in his hands. "Security check," he said with a smile, and began checking off the names of the shuttle passengers against a list. When he got to the Governor and Miss Pickerell, he shook his head. "Your names do not appear on my list."

"That's preposterous," the Governor argued. "It also indicates a high degree of inefficiency somewhere."

Miss Pickerell thought so, too.

"See here, young man," she began. She stopped when she recalled the blank television screens at the weather station.

"That's probably because the communications system between Earth and the space station has broken down," she went on. "If Mr. Humwhistel hasn't had it fixed yet, he couldn't tell anybody up here that we were coming."

"Oh," said the Governor and the young man. The young man looked very puzzled and scratched his head with his pencil. Miss Pickerell introduced herself and the Governor.

"Deputy Blakely made our reservations at the last moment. We've come to investigate the condition of the weather satellites," she explained.

"I don't imagine you'd like to keep us from carrying out that responsibility," the Governor added.

"Oh, no, Governor!" the young man said, looking somewhat dazed now. "But . . ."

"Terence!" Captain Kindle's voice suddenly called from the shuttle. "Get moving! Terence!"

The young man snapped to attention.

"That's me," he said.

He hurriedly ducked back inside the elevator. Miss Pickerell and the Governor pushed off, too, and joined him and the other passengers. The door slid shut and the elevator hummed softly as it slowly moved. Miss Pickerell couldn't decide whether they were moving upward or sideward. She was just about to ask, when the elevator stopped and the door slid open. "This is Deck 4, our living quarters," Terence explained, as the ten men and the woman with the baby left the elevator and floated out into another circular corridor. "Deck 3 is our command and control section—where we 'run' the space station. Would you like to stop there and look around?"

"Young man," began the Governor, as the elevator door shut. "We did not come here on a sightseeing trip! Take us to the weather satellite, immediately!"

"Oh, I can't do that," Terence said politely.

"Can't? What do you mean, can't?" roared the Governor.

"If you want to take a look at a weather satellite, you'll have to wait at least an hour."

"An hour!" Miss Pickerell exclaimed. "This is an emergency. We can't wait an hour."

The Governor emphatically nodded his agreement.

"I'm afraid you have no choice," Terence explained. "The polar weather satellite doesn't come near the space station before then."

"Something will have to be done about . . . ," the Governor began.

"We'd like to see your officer in charge of weather satellites immediately," Miss Pickerell stated.

"Certainly," Terence said. "Only he's not an officer. He's a professor. I'll take you to him." The elevator moved once more. "Here we are," said Terence. "Deck 4, our orbiting meteorological and life science laboratories."

He propelled himself out of the elevator. Miss Pickerell gasped as she floated across the threshold.

"Mercy!" she whispered.

"Is anything wrong, Miss Pickerell?" Terence asked anxiously.

"Oh, no!" Miss Pickerell replied, her voice quivering a little. "I . . . I just wasn't prepared for this."

It was just as though she had stepped into a tropical jungle. On either side of the circular corridor were huge, Plexiglas enclosures filled with every sort of palm tree, giant fern, and eucalyptus and hibiscus

77

bushes. Farther along the tunnel there was a section of desert cactus and another section of Northern woods—birch and pine, oak and maple trees—some of the trees dense with summer foliage and others already turning autumn colors. There were even small fields of wheat and corn, and a large vegetable garden.

"We're experimenting with plant life," Terence explained. "We're trying to learn how it will react to zero 'g.' Some of the trees seem to be doing better than others. We don't know exactly why yet."

"Soil makes a big difference," Miss Pickerell said. "If this is an experiment, I imagine you have different types of soil, as well as different kinds of plants."

Terence shrugged his shoulders. "That's not my department," he said.

"I assume the soil is all brought up from the earth," the Governor stated.

"Oh, yes," Terence replied. "The trees and everything else, too. I don't think we've tried growing anything from seed yet. But, as I said, that's not my department."

"What *is* your department?" Miss Pickerell asked, curious. "Besides meeting the space shuttle, I mean."

"Animals," Terence answered, looking very glad that she had asked.

"Animals?" Miss Pickerell repeated.

"Yes," Terence said. "We experiment with animals, too."

"What sort of experiments?" Miss Pickerell asked instantly.

"I'm studying them to see which species best adapt to a zero 'g' environment. I find out how animals like living in deep space."

"How *do* they like it?" Miss Pickerell asked.

Terence hung his head.

"I'm not sure," he admitted. "This is a new job for me. The doctor says they're all right. He checks them for blood abnormalities, calcium deficiencies, and body balance every day."

He looked hopefully at Miss Pickerell.

"Maybe you'd like to stop by and see for yourself," he suggested. "Then you can tell me which ones you think should be sent back to Earth."

"How far away are the animals?" Miss Pickerell asked.

"Straight ahead," Terence replied. "Deck 4 is divided like a pie into three pieces. The animal laboratory is in the middle."

Miss Pickerell hesitated for only a minute. Then she bobbed and floated as quickly

as she could along the corridor. Terence and the Governor bounced along with her. A pair of sliding doors opened. Miss Pickerell smiled when she looked into the one big room.

There were two medium-sized black and

white dogs, two goats, several white rabbits, a small pig, at least a dozen mice, monkeys, rats, and pigeons, and a baby lamb. They floated about in large, roomy, Plexiglas homes outfitted with tunnels and boxes where they could curl up and sleep.

"I'm glad to see you don't keep them in wire cages," Miss Pickerell said sternly.

"Oh, I couldn't do that," Terence said, "I love them too much."

Miss Pickerell went from one animal to another. She inspected them closely and made sure they had enough food and water and a soft place to rest. The baby lamb hadn't touched the milk in her bottle.

"That lamb has to go back," Miss Pickerell said decisively. "She needs her mother."

"I thought so, too," Terence said. "But she just arrived a few days ago and . . ."

"She's going back with me," Miss Pickerell said flatly. "I'll come and get her myself, before I leave. Then I'll be sure."

"Yes, Miss Pickerell," Terence said, escorting her and the Governor out of the laboratory. "I live right next door. Would you like to see my quarters? We still have plenty of time.''

He led them into a very small room before Miss Pickerell or the Governor could say anything. Miss Pickerell noticed immediately that there were no knickknacks or flowers or anything like that about. And Terence's bed looked exactly like the plant enclosures, except that his bed had a metal bar across it—to keep him from floating away, Miss Pickerell guessed. There was a chair and desk, too, and an AM-FM radio, and a television screen set into the wall.

''I have my own shower stall and bathroom,'' said Terence proudly.

''You must be very comfortable here,'' Miss Pickerell commented.

''The doctor isn't so sure,'' Terence said. ''He checks me up every day, too. He thinks something is happening to my coordination.''

''Oh?'' replied Miss Pickerell.

''Nobody's been up here for more than a few months, so far,'' Terence continued. ''The two goats and I have been here the longest. The doctor is especially interested in the three of us.''

"Oh!" Miss Pickerell and the Governor both said, looking at him with added respect.

Terence seemed embarrassed. He examined his watch.

"We're still early," he said, "but if you like, we can go on to weather satellite headquarters now."

"I prefer to be early," Miss Pickerell said.

They went out into the corridor. Directly around the next curve was another door marked Meteorology.

"That's it," said Terence. "That's where Professor Aceworthy works. I'll take you inside and introduce you."

But before Terence could even raise his hand to knock on the door, it opened from inside and the short, stout man with the bald head, whom Miss Pickerell had noticed on the space shuttle, appeared.

"Oh!" Miss Pickerell exclaimed, surprised.

"I'm the one who should be saying, 'Oh,' Miss Pickerell," he said to her in an icy tone of voice. "I have just spoken to Mr. Humwhistel via our re-established communications system. I have advised him to inform Mr. Blakely that he had no business allowing you to get on the space shuttle. We prefer to work up here without the interference of visitors who don't have the good common sense to attend to their own affairs. And you, Terence, you get right back to your job!''

Terence mumbled something unintelligible, maneuvered around, and fled.

9

A Look Through the Telescope

For an instant, Miss Pickerell and the Governor were too shocked to answer. Miss Pickerell found her voice first.

"Professor," she said, speaking very slowly and deliberately, "I think I should remind you that the possibility of a flood in Square Toe County is very much our affair. I can understand that you're upset and . . ."

"You owe Miss Pickerell an apology, Professor," the Governor interrupted loudly. "I demand it."

Professor Aceworthy suddenly looked down at his shoes. His face got very red.

"I'm sorry," he murmured. "I *am* upset. *Very.*"

"Well," the Governor said, "now that you've explained yourself, we can go on. I realize, of course, that the situation up here is a very difficult one and that . . ."

"What situation up here?" the professor asked, raising his head and his voice.

"I am referring, naturally, to the problem with the weather satellites," the Governor replied. "That's why Miss Pickerell and I . . ."

"There's nothing wrong with the weather satellites," the professor burst out. "There *can't* be anything wrong with them. That's not what's upsetting me."

Miss Pickerell and the Governor stared at each other over the professor's bald head.

"Maybe it's not very polite of me to talk this way," the professor went on. "But I have to tell someone. It's my wife. She's driving me crazy."

The Governor sighed sympathetically. Miss Pickerell gave him a sharp look. He stopped sighing immediately.

"Every time I go home for a visit, I come back here a changed man," Professor Aceworthy continued. "This last time, she told me that she's had about all she can take, worrying about me. She says she practically turns to water inside whenever I get on the space shuttle."

He looked appealingly from the Governor to Miss Pickerell and back again to the Governor.

"You didn't find it a very dangerous trip, did you?" he asked. "Or a very frightening one?"

"Not at all," the Governor replied vigorously.

Miss Pickerell said nothing.

"And she keeps giving me things to bring up here," the professor said. "Come. I'll show you."

The professor bobbed through the door into a large, wedge-shaped area. Miss Pickerell and the Governor followed close behind him. On either side of the door stood bookcases holding neatly labeled collections of magazines, books, and tapes. Next to the bookcase on the right was a huge console of buttons, gauges, lights, and switches. Several chairs were locked into place in front of the console, which also had a flat desk area extending from its left end. A telephone, a notebook, and a maneuvering gun were clamped to the desk. All very practical, thought Miss Pickerell. But what really caught her eye was the telescope. It must have been ten feet in diameter, and it stretched from the floor of the laboratory room right through the module wall and out into space. It was the biggest telescope Miss Pickerell had ever seen.

Professor Aceworthy paid no attention to any of these things. He pointed to a narrow enclosed shelf above the huge TV screen. There, packed into the rectangular space, were rows of unopened bottles of disinfectants and cans of degradable spray detergents all standing at attention.

"I don't know how many times I've told her this is a dirt-free environment up here," the professor said, looking furious again.

The Governor clucked understandingly.

"And we take great precautions *not* to track in dirt and germs from outer space," Professor Aceworthy went on. "I think what she's really worried about are the short exploring trips I occasionally make. The jump-off point is on the left there, where the wall can be unlatched."

The Governor blanched.

"Isn't that rather—er—dangerous?" he asked.

"Not when we're prepared with a safety line, enough oxygen, and a maneuvering gun," the professor told him. "But this morning I promised my wife that I wouldn't explore any more. I *had* to. It was the only way I could stop her from packing more bottles and cans."

The professor sighed deeply.

"Perhaps she's right," he said. "I'm not as young as I used to be."

Miss Pickerell was not listening very carefully. She was staring into the telescope and out into the black vastness beyond. It seemed to her that something was moving there. She couldn't exactly see anything but . . .

"Professor!" she cried. "Isn't . . . isn't that a weather satellite approaching?"

The professor squinted out into the blackness, glanced at his watch, and thumped his right fist on the palm of his left hand.

"So it is!" he said. "And, as usual, right on time."

He moved rapidly over to the telescope and peered into it.

"I suppose the two of you will want to take a look," he said, while he adjusted lenses and peered through them. "At least, I gathered as much from Mr. Humwhistel."

Miss Pickerell wished he would stop talking and concentrate on the weather satellite.

"Well, that's it," said Professor Aceworthy. He moved away from the telescope.

"It's your turn now, Miss Pickerell," he said. "Can you manage?"

Miss Pickerell stared at him incredulously.

"Do you mean," she asked, "do you mean that you've finished your inspection of the satellite?"

"Certainly," the professor said. "I know everything on there by heart. I can tell in an instant if anything's out of place. I'm sorry to disappoint you, Miss Pickerell, but all is exactly as it should be on the weather satellite."

Miss Pickerell was stunned. She also

didn't like the sarcastic note she thought she heard in the professor's voice. And she most definitely did not approve of his hasty examination of the satellite.

"I'd like to look for myself," she said stiffly.

"Please," Professor Aceworthy said, guiding her over to the lens and carefully adjusting it for her. "I'll do my best to explain while you're watching. Would you like that, Miss Pickerell? Or would you prefer to ask questions?"

"Whichever you consider best," Miss Pickerell said, thinking that either the professor was a very moody man or that he hadn't really meant to be sarcastic when he talked about her disappointment.

"Well, I'll start by talking," the professor said. "Look up in front first, Miss Pickerell."

"Yes, Professor," Miss Pickerell said, following his directions. "I'm looking."

"What do you see?" the professor asked.

"Television cameras," Miss Pickerell said.

"Right!" the professor told her. "Those are the television cameras that photograph the cloud covers and storms. And see that weather-vane sort of instrument? That gathers information about other weather factors that I won't bother to go into right now."

Miss Pickerell was able to see the television cameras so clearly, it seemed to her that she could almost hear them buzz. It was very exciting.

"And right next to them, Professor?" she asked. "Those instruments that look like the insides of my radio when the man comes to fix it? What are they?"

"Precisely what you described, Miss Pickerell," the professor said admiringly. "They are the receivers and the broadcasters that transmit the beeping radio signals about the weather to the earth."

"If they were mine, I'd clean them," Miss Pickerell exclaimed. "They're filthy, Professor!"

"You sound like my wife," the professor sighed. "Do you remember what I told her about the dust, Miss Pickerell?"

"Yes," Miss Pickerell said, sighing, too. "There isn't any dust in outer space. I knew about that before I came up here."

"Well," Professor Aceworthy said, "there's actually only one other set of items that are of interest to us on the satellite. And those, too, are exactly where they should be. Look toward the rear, now, Miss Pickerell. Do you see anything there?"

"A beehive," Miss Pickerell said.

The professor laughed.

"Not quite, Miss Pickerell," he said. "Those are solar cells. They pick up energy from the sun and transmit it to the solar batteries on the satellite. The batteries store the sun's energy as electrical energy which powers the satellite instruments."

"But they're dusty, too," Miss Pickerell protested.

"Not *dusty*," Professor Aceworthy reminded her. "Every one of those valuable instruments has been hygienically sealed. No dirt can get to the working parts."

"Humph," Miss Pickerell muttered.

She eased herself into one of the laboratory chairs and thought about the way the measuring instruments looked, while the Governor peered through the telescope and the professor stood near him, talking. She wondered whether a meteoroid might have struck the satellite. She remembered how frightened everybody had been about meteoroids when she was up on the moon. And if a meteoroid *had* hit the satellite, it could have cracked the seal and spattered dirt particles on the measuring instruments. And they were the instruments, Professor Aceworthy had said, that fed the information about weather into the computers. Now, if that information was wrong, it could be because . . .

"The Governor has asked me to show him our financial records," Professor Aceworthy's voice interrupted. "I'm sure you'd be interested in seeing them, too, Miss Pickerell."

"No, thank you, Professor," Miss Pickerell said. "I'd rather take another look through the telescope, if you don't mind."

"Not at all," the professor said. "But you'd better hurry if you want to see anything very distinctly. That satellite keeps moving, you know."

"I know," Miss Pickerell said thoughtfully.

10

A Terrible Chance

The longer Miss Pickerell looked through the telescope, the more certain she became of what needed to be done. Somebody had to get out on that satellite and clean those measuring instruments. In her opinion, nothing, absolutely nothing, could work properly with so much dirt on it. Why even her English ivy plant that stood on the sill of her bedroom window at home needed to be washed regularly. When the leaves got very dusty, they drooped.

Miss Pickerell rapidly turned over in her mind whom she might call on to take the trip to the weather satellite. The professor was out of the question. Even if he hadn't made that promise to his wife, he wouldn't go. He certainly wasn't likely to see the necessity for such a trip and he would be quick to tell her so, probably in very forceful language. She had no idea who else on the space station went out on the exploring trips that Professor Aceworthy had mentioned. Or which men made repairs. In any case, she had no time to go and look for these people. Even while she was sitting and thinking, the satellite was proceeding on its own course and moving farther and farther away from the space station.

"If I don't go this minute," Miss Pickerell exclaimed, "it may be too late to go at all."

She trembled from head to foot when she realized what she had just said.

"But what else can I do?" she asked herself, trying hard to control her panic. "I'm sure I'm right about those measuring instruments. And *somebody* has to do something to correct the situation. We can't, we simply can't have another flood in Square Toe County!"

She made her preparations as quickly as she could.

First, she chose a can of her favorite all-purpose spray detergent from the line-up on Professor Aceworthy's shelf. She looked around for something she could use to wipe off the dirt after she sprayed. There was nothing in the professor's laboratory that even looked like a dust cloth.

"That's all right," she reassured herself. "I have my handkerchief."

She immediately transferred a big, white handkerchief, folded neatly into a square, from her handbag to a pocket of her space suit. She fastened her handbag and her umbrella on one of the wall hooks beside the exit hatch. She had to push aside a number of walkie-talkies to make room for her belongings. It occurred to her as she was looking at the walkie-talkies that she might take one along.

"You never know when that sort of thing might come in handy," she thought. "And I'm sure the professor won't mind if I borrow it."

Then she checked the gauges on the oxygen tank attached to her chest. It was nearly full. She also located the turn-on valve.

"It's lucky I didn't take my space suit off," she commented, as she pulled the visor of her helmet down. She put her hands into her padded space gloves, stuffed the can of detergent into a wide chest pocket, zipped it up, and flung the walkie-talkie over her shoulder.

Last of all, she picked up the professor's maneuvering gun. She tried to recall what Euphus had once told her about how a maneuvering gun worked. It was something about how the gun thrust a space walker in the opposite direction from the way the gun was pointed. There was also something about pulling the trigger of the gun to allow the gas to escape from its nozzle.

"I remember now," Miss Pickerell breathed, feeling very relieved. "Euphus said that the gun was a small jet. What I have to do is to hold my finger on the trigger and to keep steering. I . . . I guess I'm ready to go."

She heard the professor's voice just as she was floating over to the jump-off hatch. She was fumbling with the latch when he and the Governor walked into the room.

"Miss Pickerell!" Professor Aceworthy shouted immediately. "What do you think you're doing?"

He lurched toward her. But he was too late. She had already gotten the door open and had thrust herself through the connecting chamber into outer space.

She found herself alone in a great silence. For a moment she stayed spread-eagled. Directly under her was the earth. It seemed very near.

"Miss Pickerell!" Miss Pickerell jumped at the sound. It was the professor on one of the remaining walkie-talkies. He was practically shouting into it. Miss Pickerell could hardly hear herself think. She was almost sorry she had brought a walkie-talkie.

"Come back! Come back!" the Governor's voice came screeching through on another walkie-talkie. "Miss Pickerell, please come back!"

Miss Pickerell did not take the time to answer. She maneuvered the jet of the gun until she had turned herself over and could see the earth again. It seemed to her that Square Toe Mountain lay directly beneath her. She was nearly positive, as a matter of fact. After all, if she couldn't tell, who could? She knew every slope, every curve. . . .

"If it's the weather satellite you're looking for," Professor Aceworthy called, "you'll find it on the left. I suppose there's no stopping you now."

"No, Professor," Miss Pickerell said into her walkie-talkie. "And thank you for the directions."

She moved her gun to the right. She could see the satellite clearly now. It was round and flat and looked to her like a giant hatbox. It was also not nearly as close as she had expected.

"I'll have to get there!" she told herself firmly, trying not to listen to the way her heart was pounding.

But she couldn't seem to make much progress. She kept her eyes fixed steadily on the satellite. And she steered very carefully in the correct direction. The satellite remained as far away as ever, however.

"I . . . I don't know what to do," she whispered, frantically.

Then she remembered that the satellite was moving, too. She would just have to go faster and catch up with it. The Governor and the professor were both shouting at her on their walkie-talkies. They made a jumble of sounds. She gave up trying to understand them. She concentrated on her maneuvering gun. She did not let go of the trigger for an instant. And as she pointed, she could almost feel the thrusts that moved her nearer and nearer.

"Why, I'm practically there," she cried out jubilantly. "Just a few more thrusts and . . ."

"And now that you are," the professor interrupted, "just what do you expect to do?"

"Get on, of course," Miss Pickerell replied promptly, "and clean the dirt off the measuring instruments."

"You're mad!" Professor Aceworthy screamed. "You and my wife!"

"Why don't you just clean the satellite up on the outside, Miss Pickerell?" the Governor pleaded. "I'm sure you could do a great job with the outside."

"But I have to get *on*," Miss Pickerell explained. "I have to clean the meteorite dirt particles off the measuring instruments so that they can feed the correct weather information into the computers. It's the only . . ."

"What dirt particles did you say?" Professor Aceworthy suddenly shouted.

"Meteorite dirt particles," Miss Pickerell repeated, impatiently. She could almost touch the weather satellite now. And she wished the Governor and the professor would keep still.

But the professor's voice came through on the walkie-talkie again. He spoke very quietly now.

"Miss Pickerell," he said, "you may or may not be right. But I must seriously advise you to turn right around and come back to the space station."

Miss Pickerell was outraged.

"Professor Aceworthy," she said, "if I've come this far to try to prevent another flood in Square Toe County, I'm certainly going to finish the job. I'm climbing up on the satellite right now."

"Oh!" the Governor wailed.

"Miss Pickerell," the professor said, talking still more quietly now, "I don't wish to alarm you. But it is my duty to warn you that your maneuvering gun holds a limited amount of compressed gas. You are taking a chance when you climb up on that satellite.''

Miss Pickerell's heart stood still. She hesitated, but only for an instant. She reached out her arm, took a firm hold of one of the hand grips, and pulled herself to the satellite.

''I'll keep track of the distance between satellite and space station,'' she told the professor.

''But can you accurately estimate the amount of gas you will need to get back to the space station?'' the professor asked ominously. ''You're still taking a terrible chance, Miss Pickerell!''

''I'll . . . I'll risk it,'' Miss Pickerell said, talking more to herself than to the professor, as she resolutely climbed up onto the satellite.

11

On the Weather Satellite

Miss Pickerell noticed immediately that
the weather satellite was a very busy place.
The television cameras, the receivers, the
broadcasters, and the measuring instruments were all humming and snapping and
small, bright-colored lights kept flashing on
and off all around her. A tape recorder
hooked in next to the television cameras
made loud whirring noises as it revolved.
And a number of Geiger counters that
leaned against the tape recorder kept click-
ing away. She hadn't expected quite so
much activity. It all made her a little dizzy.
She closed her eyes.

"This is no time for napping, Miss Pickerell," Professor Aceworthy's voice warned her over the walkie-talkie.

"I was *not* napping," Miss Pickerell replied, opening her eyes indignantly and feeling even dizzier than before. "I . . . I was just thinking."

"I was under the impression that you had done all your thinking before you started out on this idiotic venture," Professor Aceworthy replied. "Keep your mind on your cleaning tasks, Miss Pickerell, and get going."

"Yes, Professor," Miss Pickerell said meekly.

Her head was swimming. She leaned over the tape recorder. She seemed to feel a little better when she didn't look into space.

"Miss Pickerell!" the professor shouted. "What are you doing now?"

"This . . . this tape recorder . . . ," Miss Pickerell faltered, not knowing what else to say. She certainly was not going to tell the professor how she felt.

"If you must know," Professor Aceworthy said, "we feed the data it collects into the computer, too. But . . ."

"Please, Miss Pickerell," the Governor interrupted, "please do what you said you were going to do, quickly."

"Yes, Governor, I will," Miss Pickerell answered.

She took the can of detergent out of the wide front pocket of her space suit and removed her handkerchief from a smaller side pocket. Even this little motion made her stomach feel as though it was turning somersaults.

"I must be hungry," she told herself reassuringly. "After all, I haven't had anything to eat since breakfast."

She decided to spray the entire front of the weather satellite before she went on. Everything on the satellite seemed to be some sort of measuring instrument, really.

"Anyway, a good cleaning can't hurt," she thought. *Sssspt*, went the spray. "Forevermore!" exclaimed Miss Pickerell. The jet of detergent had thrust her several feet from the satellite.

"I'll simply have to remember to hold on when I spray," she told herself firmly.

She repointed her gun and found herself hovering over the Geiger counters.

"I suppose you're wondering about the

Geiger counters now, Miss Pickerell," the professor said.

"No," Miss Pickerell told him. "I know about those. They detect radiation."

"Well, then," the professor said, irritably.

"Miss Pickerell," the Governor added, "I must insist that you proceed with your plan and return to the space station at once."

Miss Pickerell nodded.

"Please," she said, raising her eyes to the stars and making sure that she was not speaking into the walkie-talkie, "please don't let me get sick right now. I *have* to fix those instruments and avoid a terrible flood in Square Toe County."

She forced herself over to the measuring instruments. There were six of them. She didn't know whether it was because she wasn't feeling well but they reminded her very much of huge fever thermometers. They stood upright and had numbers marked on them at spaced intervals. Little red lights showed halfway up on each instrument.

All six of the measuring instruments were covered with dirt particles of various sizes and shapes. The instruments also stood in heaps of dirt particles. Some of the particles were so big, they looked like rocks.

"I could put one of them in my pocket and take it home with me," Miss Pickerell reflected. "I could add it to my rock collection."

On reconsideration, she decided against the idea. She remembered that people who brought objects back from outer space had to stay in quarantine. She didn't want to have to do that. She thought of Pumpkins and her cow and wished she were back with them this very minute.

"Miss Pickerell!" Professor Aceworthy's warning voice sounded again.

"Yes, yes, Professor," Miss Pickerell said, spraying quickly and beginning to feel a little irritated herself. What did the professor want? She hadn't been up on the satellite for more than a minute or two at the most. She looked toward the space station and breathed a sigh of relief. She still hadn't moved too far away.

Her eyes were hurting now. She paid no attention. As long as she was able to keep them open and did not feel too dizzy to do

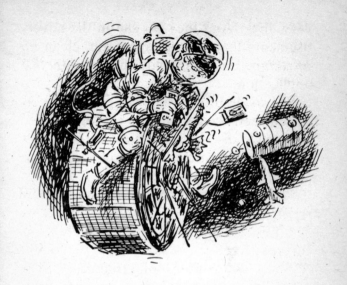

what she had to do, she was grateful. She carefully wiped the measuring instruments with her handkerchief. It was black when she finished. And the instruments were still dirty. She frowned.

"This spray detergent certainly isn't all they say it is in the advertisements, Governor," she called out.

"Isn't it?" the Governor replied.

"Miss Pickerell!" the professor shouted.

"It works all right in my house," she said to herself, as she sprayed and wiped again. "But then, I never let my house get very dirty. And they *do* say in the advertisements that this detergent can clean up *anything,* no matter how filthy, with one application.''

She made up her mind to change detergents when she got back to Earth. She also decided to discuss the subject with the new Bureau of Consumer Affairs in Square Toe County.

"Miss Pickerell!" the professor shouted again.

"Yes, I know," Miss Pickerell answered.

She took another look around.

"I'll just have time for one more application," she thought, as she rapidly sprayed the six instruments, waited one second, wiped them as best she could with her handkerchief, and examined them closely. They looked a little better. Two seemed almost clean. Miss Pickerell patted them the way she sometimes patted Pumpkins when she was particularly pleased with him. Then she noticed something.

"Forevermore!" she burst out.

"What is it?" the professor's voice boomed. "Miss Pickerell! Miss Pickerell!"

"Yes, Professor, I hear you," Miss

Pickerell said. "Something has happened out here."

"What?" the Governor screamed. "What has happened?"

"That little red light on the weather instruments . . . ," Miss Pickerell began.

"Yes, Miss Pickerell?" the professor asked.

"On two of the measuring instruments," Miss Pickerell said, "it has moved to a different place."

"Oh?" the professor exclaimed.

"Now, if I could give the other four instruments one more spray, they might . . . ," she said.

"You will do no such thing!" the professor interrupted.

"We absolutely forbid it!" the Governor shouted.

"Miss Pickerell," Professor Aceworthy continued, "you probably have just enough gas in the gun cartridge to make it back to the space station, if you start now. If you delay . . ."

His voice trailed off. Miss Pickerell knew what he meant. She glanced at the widening distance. She was afraid the professor was right. She put the spray can and her handkerchief back into the front pocket. Then she steered herself quickly to the edge of the weather satellite. Her head spinning like a top in full motion and her eyes half closed, she slid off into outer space again.

12

The Blinding Light

This time, Miss Pickerell found herself looking straight ahead at the space station. She was very grateful. She felt much too tired to turn herself around. Her eyes kept closing. What was even worse, every time she opened them, her head began to reel.

"But this is ridiculous," she told herself, as she steadied her shaking finger on the jet gun nozzle and tried to concentrate on steering herself as fast as she could toward the space station. She decided to think about pleasant things that might help take her mind off the dizziness.

The first thing she thought of was her big, comfortable bed on Square Toe Farm.

She imagined the feel of the crisp, white sheets and of the soft, goosedown pillows. She could almost see the pink and white afghan lying at the foot of the bed. She remembered that she had used number seven needles when she knitted the squares of the afghan. They had come out just right. Miss Pickerell smiled. Her eyes closed.

"To the left, Miss Pickerell!" Professor Aceworthy's voice blared on the walkie-talkie. "Steer to the left. You're way off course. What's the matter with you, Miss Pickerell?"

"Nothing, Professor," Miss Pickerell whispered.

She felt horrified. If she did not concentrate, she would just wander and use up all the compressed gas before she could get anywhere near the space station. Then she would stay whirling around in space forever, or whatever the time was, like one more artificial satellite.

She was very glad now that she had taken the walkie-talkie along with her. It had probably saved her life. She wished that the professor would keep on talking to her. It would only be for a little while. The space station still seemed terribly far away. But, if she moved fast . . .

"Professor," she asked, in as energetic a tone of voice as she could manage, "has any new contact been made with Earth?"

"Not yet," the professor said. "I have the communication boys in my team working on it."

"Good!" Miss Pickerell exclaimed.

"Why?" the professor asked. "What do you expect to hear?"

"I was wondering . . . ," Miss Pickerell said, vaguely.

"Wondering?" the professor asked.

"Well, those little red lights *did* change position," Miss Pickerell said. "I was thinking that it could mean something, maybe that the meteorite particles were clogging something before and that . . ."

"Never mind all that now, Miss Pickerell!" the Governor called out. "I'll take care of it. You must pay strict attention to your maneuvering gun."

"Yes, Governor," Miss Pickerell said, raising her head a little to look at him. The motion made her feel dizzy again. She lowered her head quickly and looked down at the earth.

"I'm practically positive that's Square Toe Mountain right underneath me," she thought.

She had no idea what time it was. As she looked at Earth, she could see that part of it was in darkness and part of it was still light. Square Toe County was in the light— Daylight Saving Zone. It was probably late in the afternoon. Everybody on the farm would be busy doing late afternoon chores. Somebody would be milking the cow. Rosemary would be helping her mother get supper. Or she would be feeding Pumpkins. Or, at her father's insistence, she might be practicing the piano. Miss Pickerell did not think much of Rosemary's piano playing. As a matter of fact, Miss Pickerell went so far as to consider Rosemary's weekly piano lessons a total waste of money. Rosemary herself had said that she preferred to learn to play the guitar. One of her friends played folk songs on the guitar. Rosemary liked folk . . .

"Oh!" Miss Pickerell gasped. A blinding flash of light struck her full in the eyes. She automatically brought her right hand up in front of her face. Sudden fear twisted her stomach when she felt her hand unconsciously loosen its grip on the jet gun. As fast as she could, she clenched her fingers around it again. She rubbed her left hand across her eyes.

"No!" she whispered. "No! No!"

"What is it, Miss Pickerell?" Professor Aceworthy called. "You're going in the wrong direction."

"I . . . I can't see," Miss Pickerell shouted. "I can't see in front of me."

"What!" the Governor exclaimed.

"My . . . my eyes," Miss Pickerell tried to explain. "They . . . they feel . . . dazzled, I think. By some light . . . They . . . they can't focus. . . ."

"I'll guide you, Miss Pickerell," the professor said instantly. "Just listen to me and do everything I say. Can you hear me, Miss Pickerell?"

"Yes, Professor," Miss Pickerell said.

"Put your right hand back where it was," the professor said. "That's good. Hold tight now, Miss Pickerell, and point the gun to the left."

Miss Pickerell felt numb. But she did as she was told.

"Now, pull the trigger."

"Ohhh!" Miss Pickerell felt sure she was going to scream.

"Professor," she said in a very weak voice. "The trigger on the gun is stuck!"

"That's done it," groaned the Governor.

"Keep calm, Miss Pickerell. Keep calm," ordered Professor Aceworthy. "And you, too, Governor. And you, Miss Pickerell, don't worry about a thing. You're just a couple of feet or so from the air lock now."

"The air lock?" Miss Pickerell asked.

"I'll explain about the air lock later," the professor said. "Do you still have that can of detergent?"

"Of course!" Miss Pickerell fairly shouted. And a sudden rush of confidence came to her as she removed the can from her front pocket.

"Good! Good!" Professor Aceworthy went on. "Push the spray button. Now spray to your left, Miss Pickerell. A little to the right now. That's it. That's it."

Miss Pickerell could almost hear her own anxious breathing as she held tight to the can of detergent and kept thrusting her-

self forward. In her ears, there was also a
loud, steady hissing sound that she hadn't
noticed before. Her lips trembled.

She blinked her eyes. It seemed to her
that she could see a little better than before. That made her feel a bit more optimistic. She decided that the hissing sound
probably came from her rubberized space
suit. Most likely, she hadn't been paying
any attention to it until now. She remembered the television program she had once
watched where an astronaut talked about

the pressurizing, breathing, cooling, and drying systems that were built into a space suit.

"Just a few inches now, Miss Pickerell," the professor said. "You're nearly here."

"Yes, Professor," Miss Pickerell said, thinking that at this moment a few inches seemed more like a few miles. She was finding it very difficult to keep on feeling optimistic. Her eyes had shooting pains in them now. She could hardly breathe.

"I must be brave," she told herself, as she felt the final spray of detergent leave the can. "I must . . ."

Strong hands suddenly supported her under her arms. She felt a chair being placed beneath her. She heard the professor say, "Bravo, Miss Pickerell!" She tried to thank him for all the help he had given her. Her voice cracked when she began to talk. Her head fell forward. She lost consciousness.

13

Back to Earth

The first person Miss Pickerell saw when she opened her eyes was the Governor. He was at her side holding a bottle of smelling salts under her nose. The ammonia in it almost made her sneeze. She pushed the bottle aside.

"Where . . . where did you find that?" she asked, referring to the smelling salts.

The Governor looked a little embarrassed.

"My wife gave it to me," he said. "She insisted that I take it along with me if I was going up into outer space. She's . . . she's a very old-fashioned woman."

"Not at all," Miss Pickerell said, coming to her defense immediately. "She was quite right about the smelling salts."

"Well . . . ," the Governor said, smiling.

"She also bakes the best six-egg sponge cake in Square Toe County," Miss Pickerell went on. "I tasted it at the last state fair."

"Well . . . ," the Governor said again, beaming this time.

"And I don't think she would have fainted the way I did," Miss Pickerell added apologetically.

"You didn't mean to faint," the Governor reassured her. "You are a very brave lady, Miss Pickerell. I don't know another who would have undertaken what you did."

"Somebody *had* to," Miss Pickerell said practically.

The Governor nodded.

"I'm sorry I gave you and the professor so much trouble when that light flashed in my eyes," she went on. "I can't even imagine what it was."

"The professor can't figure it out, either," the Governor said, sighing. "But he has all the scientists on the space station and at ground control hard at work tracking down the cause. It's a real mystery."

Miss Pickerell was suddenly aware of a great deal of noise and confusion going on around her. Scientists crowded around the telescope, taking turns peering through it. Technicians were monitoring masses of information coming from the computer console. Television screens were on and flickering—one of them showed a fuzzy rolling picture of Mr. Humwhistel. He seemed very upset by the news being relayed to him from outer space. But the one person Miss Pickerell wanted most to talk to was missing.

"Where is Professor Aceworthy?" she asked anxiously.

"Preparing some soup for you," the Governor replied. "There's nothing like good, hot soup to put you on your feet again. My wife always says that."

Privately, Miss Pickerell agreed. Still, she did not think that the professor should be spending his time on soup at this moment. It was more important to find out what was going on in Square Toe County. She told the Governor as much.

"But we know about that now," the Governor said, just as Professor Aceworthy drifted in. The professor was carrying a fiberboard tray with two plastic tubes clamped to it—one was steaming and the other was filled with brownish cracker cubes. Miss Pickerell felt very attracted to the soup, even though she was not at all sure how she should go about eating it. The professor slid the tray into the holding grooves on the desk in front of her. "Just put the flexible straw in your mouth, and squeeze," Professor Aceworthy explained.

"Thank you, Professor," she said, between gulps.

"Not at all," the professor said. "I'm glad you like it."

Miss Pickerell took several more sips, then put down the half-finished soup tube and looked intently at the professor. "I'm very anxious to know what's happening in Square Toe County."

"Well," said Professor Aceworthy, "we're certain that strange flash of light came from the top of Square Toe Mountain.

"But what about the dam?" Miss Pickerell asked.

"Please go on eating, Miss Pickerell," Professor Aceworthy said. "The Governor and I will tell you all about it."

But neither the professor nor the Governor went on to say anything. The Governor leaned up against the console. The professor floated slowly around the room. Miss Pickerell stared at them.

"The news is mixed," Professor Aceworthy said, finally. "My boys have just left the console board. They talked to Mr. Humwhistel."

Miss Pickerell stood up. The empty soup tube bounced into the air as she pushed herself away from the desk.

"There *has* been a flood!" she said. "That's it, isn't it, Governor? A flood?"

"Almost," the Governor admitted.

"It's been raining hard ever since you left Square Toe County," Professor Aceworthy added. "And the storm seems to be getting worse."

Miss Pickerell sank weakly back into her chair.

"But the weather forecast is for rain

now," the Governor said quickly. "The forecast became accurate as soon as you pushed off from the satellite. Before, it went haywire whenever it passed directly over Square Toe Mountain. How fortunate, Miss Pickerell, that you insisted on going out there to clean the instruments. But now there's this strange light that . . ."

"The dam?" Miss Pickerell interrupted.

"Yes, yes, Miss Pickerell," the Governor said. "I've given an order for the gate to be opened instantly."

"Well, then . . . ," Miss Pickerell said, breathing normally again.

The Governor did not answer. He avoided looking at her.

"What the Governor is afraid of," Professor Aceworthy said slowly, "is that his order may have come too late. The water in the reservoir was nearly up to the top when the weather forecast changed. And, as I told you, the storm seems to be at its height now."

"I must go back to Earth, Miss Pickerell," the Governor said. "I must go immediately. In case of disaster emergencies . . ."

He did not finish. He did not need to.

Miss Pickerell understood only too well.

"The space shuttle is here," Professor Aceworthy stated. "You and the Governor can leave immediately, if you like, Miss Pickerell. Captain Kindle will give you fresh oxygen tanks."

"Shall we go, Miss Pickerell?" the Governor asked.

"As soon as I get the lamb," Miss Pickerell said.

"The lamb? What lamb?" Professor Aceworthy asked.

"The baby lamb who is too young to be up here," Miss Pickerell said. "I promised I would take her back to her mother."

The professor looked dumbfounded.

"The lamb that Terence is taking care of, Professor," the Governor explained. "Miss Pickerell saw her when we were . . ."

"I'll see to it that the lamb is waiting for you on the shuttle when you get there, Miss Pickerell," the professor stated. "It's the least I can do for you in the way of gratitude."

"Gratitude?" Miss Pickerell asked.

"For tolerating my bad manners," Professor Aceworthy said. "And for teaching me not to be such a know-it-all. If you hadn't made that trip to the satellite, we would never have discovered that strange beam of light."

"Oh!" Miss Pickerell replied.

"I'm afraid we'd better go now, Miss Pickerell," the Governor reminded her. "I don't like to look at the dark side but . . ."

Miss Pickerell told him that she was ready. She said good-bye to Professor Aceworthy, and wished him luck in finding the source of the terrible light. Then she glided solemnly along the corridor with the Governor. She tried hard not to think of what might be awaiting them in Square Toe County. But she couldn't put her mind on anything else. This time, she did not even notice that they had entered the elevator, descended three decks, and stopped. It came almost as a shock to her when Terence handed her the lamb at the entrance to the space shuttle. But she held out her arms for the animal immediately.

"Where's her space suit?" she asked.

"I have everything," Captain Kindle said, coming toward them. "Another oxygen tank for you, Miss Pickerell! And one for you, Governor! And one animal space suit, complete with tank!''

The lamb bleated faintly when Captain Kindle put the helmet on her head. Miss Pickerell told her that everything would be all right soon. Terence gave Miss Pickerell the address of the farm where the lamb's mother lived. The Governor asked Captain Kindle whether the trip would be very rough because of the storm.

"As soon as we begin to approach Earth, it will be," Captain Kindle said. "Let's hope it will have calmed down a little by the time we get there."

"I'm with you on that," the Governor said.

Miss Pickerell noticed that the Governor neither ate nor slept on the return trip. He did not say a word to her, either. He sat and sighed. Miss Pickerell did not know what to say to him. She spent most of her time talking to the lamb.

"If your mother doesn't want you," she told her, "I'll take you home with me."

Captain Kindle's voice suddenly filled the cabin.

"Good news, ladies and gentlemen!" he

said. "The weather on the ground is clear. We'll come down in between storms."

Miss Pickerell looked at the Governor and smiled. Even the lamb seemed happier in her lap.

In a few minutes, the stewardess came down the aisle, announcing that they were getting ready to land. Everyone returned to their reclining seats and fastened the straps.

"It won't be so bad this time," she stopped to tell Miss Pickerell. "The retro-rockets will blast, slowing down the space shuttle. And you will feel a force pushing against your back. But at least you'll know what to expect."

Miss Pickerell wished that the stewardess would keep her thoughts to herself.

The Governor looked grim as he adjusted the button on his oxygen tank. Miss Pickerell knew what he was thinking. She was having the same fears. Her mind was so full of the horrors they might find when they got to the dam, she hardly felt the gravity at all when they landed.

The lamb bleated gratefully when Miss Pickerell took off her spacesuit. Miss Pickerell sighed with relief, too, when she stepped out of the clumsy garment and climbed shakily off the shuttle. She looked around.

It was seven o'clock in Square Toe County. The mountain tops mingled with the soft, white clouds above them. The valley lay serenely between the heights, the rays of the sun just beginning to disappear from its green surfaces. The rain had stopped. The air smelled sharply fresh and clean. Miss Pickerell took a deep breath.

"Nothing can be wrong on an evening like this," she whispered.

"We'll see," the Governor, who had heard her, answered.

14

At the Reservoir

Miss Pickerell was so glad to be back on Earth that she did not notice at first how deserted the space field was. When she *did* look around, she saw that nobody except the man who helped people get off the space shuttle was there. The loneliness made Miss Pickerell shiver a little. But before she had a chance to talk about this to the Governor, she saw a black limousine with the state flag flying over it come speeding toward the runway. And almost at the same moment she heard the distant drone of a helicopter overhead.

The droning quickly grew louder. The

helicopter came closer. It whirled to a sudden stop right in front of Miss Pickerell just as the limousine ground to a halt at her feet. Miss Pickerell looked questioningly up at the Governor.

"I ordered the helicopter when I spoke to Earth from the space station," he explained. "I knew you'd be anxious to get to the reservoir as fast as possible. By helicopter, you'll be there in no time, Miss Pickerell."

"What about you, Governor?" Miss Pickerell asked.

The Governor sighed wearily.

"I'm afraid I must go and make a statement to the press," he said. "The reporters are all waiting at the weather station. Of course, if you'd like to come along . . ."

"No, thank you, Governor," said Miss Pickerell, hastily. "I'd rather see what's happening at the reservoir."

She climbed into the waiting helicopter. The lamb began to tremble as the propellers started whirling again. She hid her face in the folds of Miss Pickerell's dress.

Miss Pickerell was just leaning over her and telling her that she was a good girl when the helicopter landed on the grass beside the reservoir headquarters. Miss Pickerell stood up on tiptoe to see the reservoir. She gasped.

It looked as though the entire population of Square Toe County had gathered around the reservoir. And everybody was very busy piling sandbags, one on top of another, at its edge. Miss Pickerell knew why the minute she noticed the water in the reservoir. It was nearly up to the very top. One more drop of rain and the reservoir would overflow. The double circle of sandbags was making the reservoir walls a little higher, holding back the flood for just a little while longer.

"Forevermore!" Miss Pickerell whispered.

Hugging the lamb close, she jumped off the helicopter, and walked quickly toward the reservoir. People with worried faces glanced up from their sandbags for a moment and tried to smile. They made room for her to pass. She stopped when she saw the dark line that ran around the reservoir, just above the water.

"What's that?" she asked breathlessly.

"That's where the water was a little

while ago," said a familiar voice behind her.

"Then the gate has been opened," Miss Pickerell breathed. "The water *is* flowing out slowly and safely into Square Toe River."

"Very slowly," the man behind her said.

Miss Pickerell turned around. Mr. Kettelson, looking grayer and sadder than ever, was standing there.

"The sandbags are a protection until some of the water has a chance to empty," he went on.

"What a perfectly wonderful idea!" Miss Pickerell exclaimed.

"It was mine," Mr. Kettelson said.

"That was very practical of you," Miss Pickerell said admiringly.

"Machines can't do everything," Mr. Kettelson replied.

"I never said they could," Miss Pickerell told him. "If I ever gave you that impression, Mr. Kettelson, I . . ."

She stopped in mid-sentence.

"What is it, Miss Pickerell?" Mr. Kettelson asked anxiously.

"Nothing," Miss Pickerell said. She

137

thought she had felt a drop of rain on her nose. But she wasn't entirely sure. And she was not about to spoil Mr. Kettelson's pleasure for no good reason.

"I hope you realize," Mr. Kettelson went on, "that you saved us all from a terrible flood in Square Toe County. Why, even your cow could have been drowned and . . ."

"Oh!" Miss Pickerell interrupted. There was no question about the rain now. She had felt two more drops. Mr. Kettelson had felt them, too. He was looking at her in dismay.

"I'll bring down some more bags," he said, in a low, hopeless voice. "I have some extras on my truck. We'll need every one of them."

"Yes," Miss Pickerell said tonelessly.

She felt very tired as she watched the water flow slowly out the open gate in the dam. The rain was coming down harder and harder. Everybody had become very quiet. Most people were piling more sandbags on the two rows that now ringed the reservoir. A few persons simply stared mournfully at the water.

"Whatever I did was all probably too late to be of any use," Miss Pickerell whispered, half to herself and half to the frightened lamb she was cradling in her arms. "We must do something! We must . . ."

At just that moment, Miss Pickerell saw the lady reporter from the *Square Toe Gazette*. Miss Pickerell recognized her right away. At this time of year, the lady reporter always wore a big picture hat. The Governor and his wife were close behind her. And following them were at least twenty reporters and photographers and radio and television interviewers. The reporters all had pencils and pads of paper in their hands. The photographers and interviewers carried cameras and microphones. They advanced on Miss Pickerell and began asking questions at once.

"Are you going to keep the lamb?"

"Will she be a friend for your cow?"

"Just what did you do on the weather satellite?"

"How did it feel to take a walk in space?"

"Were you afraid?"

"What caused that blinding light?"

"Turn to the right, please!"

"One more picture, full face! Hold the lamb up in front!"

"One with the Governor, now! That's it!"

Miss Pickerell shrank back as the cameras clicked all around her. She said nothing. The lady reporter walked over to her.

"I can understand how you feel, Miss Pickerell," she said. "You're probably much too excited to say anything right now. What you need is a nice cup of tea and . . ."

"Not really," Miss Pickerell said qui-

141

etly. "I'm just too worried to *want* to say anything."

"Worried about what?" the lady reporter asked, starting to write immediately.

"Why, the flood, of course!" Miss Pickerell said in amazement. "It's raining again and the water in the reservoir is practically up to the top and . . ."

"More water is flowing out through the gate than is coming down," a young man with a camera burst out. "You saved us just in time, Miss Pickerell."

"Besides, it's going to stop raining any minute now," a TV writer called out to her.

"How do you know?" Miss Pickerell asked despondently.

"I just listened to the weather forecast," the man said. "And look! Look straight up, Miss Pickerell! The sun is coming out."

Miss Pickerell fixed her eyes on the spot in the sky where the man was pointing. It looked more to her like a cloud than a patch of sunlight. She expressed her opinion frankly.

"I'll make a bargain with you, Miss Pickerell," the man said. "If the sun comes out within the next five minutes, I get an interview and your exclusive story. Is it a deal?''

''Well,'' Miss Pickerell said, smiling a little, ''I don't make deals. But if that sun really does come out from behind the clouds, I'll be ready to do almost anything!''

15

Euphus Solves a Mystery

The sun made its way through the clouds in less than five minutes. The people of Square Toe County took one long look, breathed one great sigh of relief, and laid down their sandbags. They began to cheer. The governor led the cheering.

"Two! Four! Six! Eight! Who do we appreciate?" he shouted.

And everybody shouted back, "Miss Pickerell! Miss Pickerell! Miss Pickerell!"

Miss Pickerell saw Deputy Blakely in the crowd and Mr. Esticott and the Governor's wife. It seemed strange, though, to Miss Pickerell that she couldn't see her

brother and his family anywhere. She said
as much to Mr. Kettelson while he was
driving her home in his truck. Mr. Kettelson said that he hadn't seen them around,
either. For the rest of the bumpy ride up
Square Toe Mountain Road, Miss Pickerell sat in silence.

When they reached the farm, Miss Pickerell thanked him and told him she couldn't
have stopped the flood without his help and
his sandbags. Mr. Kettelson's face broke
into a smile. It made him look like a much
younger man. He was still smiling as he
drove away.

Only Rosemary, Pumpkins, and the cow
were waiting on the front lawn to greet her.
Miss Pickerell hugged them all and introduced the lamb. Pumpkins sniffed the lamb
and meowed softly. The cow made no
comment. "I'm very glad you're back,"
said Rosemary. "And I like the lamb."

"Yes," agreed Miss Pickerell, "I've
grown fond of her too." Then she looked
intently at her niece and asked, "Where
are your brothers and sisters?"

While Miss Pickerell put the lamb down
and urged her to eat some grass, Rosemary
told Miss Pickerell that the two youngest

children had gone off in the station wagon with their parents.

"Where to?" Miss Pickerell asked.

"Harry and Homer went with Dwight in your car," Rosemary went on.

"Where to?" Miss Pickerell repeated. "And where's Euphus?"

Rosemary patted the lamb.

"I think the lamb ought to have some milk," she said.

Miss Pickerell was beginning to feel a little uneasy. Rosemary had not asked her a single question about the trip to outer space. And she was definitely trying to keep from answering the questions that Miss Pickerell asked. Miss Pickerell stared at her. Rosemary lowered her eyes. She kept them fixed on her brown sandals.

"Euphus has disappeared," she mumbled, at last.

"Impossible!" Miss Pickerell said immediately. "He has more sense."

"I don't know! I don't know!" Rosemary replied, bursting into tears. "It's hours since he left. He didn't say where he was going. He just rode off on Mr. Humwhistel's bicycle, the old one that he left in your barn when he . . ."

Rosemary's voice was beginning to sound a little hysterical.

"Yes, yes," Miss Pickerell said, holding her close and trying to figure out what to do next. "Let's go inside and sit down and you can tell me all about it."

"Yes," Rosemary said, sniffling. "I'll heat some milk for the lamb."

Rosemary picked up the lamb. Pumpkins followed Rosemary into the house. The cow followed Miss Pickerell as far as the steps to the kitchen. Miss Pickerell explained to the cow that she would take her to her pasture as soon as she could. Rosemary put some milk into a saucepan. Miss Pickerell sat at the kitchen table, trying desperately to put her thoughts in order. "First things first," she told herself.

"We must start from the beginning," she said to Rosemary, as she got up out of her chair because she couldn't sit still any more. "Yes, we must start from the very beginning."

"You sound like a lady detective," Rosemary laughed, in a voice that sounded very high-pitched again. Miss Pickerell wondered what she would do if Rosemary really *had* hysterics.

"What was Euphus doing before he left the house?" she asked sternly.

"Listening to the radio," Rosemary replied. "We all were."

"Just what was he listening to?" Miss Pickerell went on.

"What we were all listening to," Rosemary said, "to some scientists on the air. They were trying o understand the reasons for the blinding light. They had all kinds of ideas."

"Oh?" Miss Pickerell asked.

"Euphus didn't agree with any of them," Rosemary continued. "He said that he was waiting for them to get to *his* theory."

"Ah!" Miss Pickerell exclaimed. "Now we are on the track, I think. Just what was Euphus' theory?"

"He didn't say," Rosemary stated. "All he kept saying was 'giant laser beam' over and over again."

Miss Pickerell couldn't imagine what Euphus' theory about the giant laser beam might be. But she felt reasonably certain of one thing. If Euphus had any questions about the laser beam, he would go and find the answers.

"I must get to the astronomical observatory," Miss Pickerell said, straightening her hat and picking up her handbag and umbrella from the kitchen table.

"The observatory is closed," Rosemary said. "They shut it this morning at the beginning of the storm."

"That doesn't matter," Miss Pickerell said, walking resolutely toward the door.

"You can't get there," Rosemary said. "You haven't got a car."

Miss Pickerell turned around.

"Well, if I haven't got a car, I know eomeone who does," she said as she marched straight to the telephone.

The Sheriff was very cooperative when Miss Pickerell explained the situation to him.

"Thank you, Sheriff," Miss Pickerell said. "I appreciate this very much."

"Not at all, Miss Pickerell!" the Sheriff replied. "Not at all!"

Miss Pickerell paced the floor until she heard the Sheriff's car pull in to her farm. She did not wait for him to come to the door. She grabbed her umbrella and handbag, told Rosemary not to worry, and ran to join the Sheriff in his car.

"I believe my nephew Euphus has gone

to the observatory,'' she explained, as the
Sheriff eased the car over the muddy ruts
the rain had cut in the dirt road. ''He was
last seen riding Mr. Humwhistel's old bicycle.''

''Bad time to be out riding a bicycle.
Blinding rain and potholes. No telling what
might have happened,'' said the Sheriff,
staring grimly at the road which was growing naint in the approaching dusk. He
switched on the headlights.

Miss Pickerell stiffened in her seat. The
lights had picked up the abandoned re-
mains of a bicycle sprawled on its side in
the weeds.

The Sheriff and Miss Pickerell lunged
from the car and ran to the fallen bike.

''Euphus!'' Miss Pickerell called. There
was no answer.

''Is this Humwhistel's bike?'' the Sheriff
asked. Miss Pickerell bent down for a close
look at the rusty machine.

''It is,'' said Miss Pickerell. ''And Euphus . . .''

''Well,'' said the Sheriff, straightening
up, ''we're not far from the observatory.
No reason he couldn't have made it the
rest of the way on foot—if he wasn't hurt.''

Miss Pickerell felt a wave of terror rise from her stomach. They got back into the Sheriff's car. She leaned forward impatiently. The seatbelt held her fast.

"We're almost there," said the Sheriff.

Up ahead loomed the huge domed observatory building. And caught in the bright headlights of the Sheriff's car were two figures running down the road.

"Stop!" ordered Miss Pickerell.

The Sheriff hit the brakes.

"It's Euphus!" cried Miss Pickerell. "And Mr. Humwhistel!"

"So it is," exclaimed the Sheriff.

Miss Pickerell felt so weak with relief that she nearly cried when she held Euphus in her arms. He struggled out as fast as he could. He looked embarrassed. Mr. Humwhistel looked red as a beet and was gasping for breath. "It's my fault . . . all my fault," he kept repeating.

"What's all your fault?" Miss Pickerell asked.

"That blinding light in your eyes . . . the trouble with the satellite . . . the near flood . . ." sputtered Mr. Humwhistel. "And it was Euphus who thought of . . ."

"The laser beam," Euphus broke in. "The laser was on. I knew it. I knew it all the time."

"He's right," said Mr. Humwhistel. "I should have told the man in charge to turn the laser off before he closed the observatory."

"He should have thought of it himself," Miss Pickerell replied promptly.

"He's not the man who is usually in charge," Mr. Humwhistel said. "That man is on vacation."

"Everybody's always on vacation," the Sheriff commented. "They'll think I'm on vacation, too, if I don't report in and get you folks home."

The ride home was most relaxing. Miss Pickerell looked forward to a quiet evening alone on her farm. She made plans as the Sheriff drove along the winding mountain road. She thought she would have a cup of tea and finish her crossword puzzle. She was just wondering how the word PEACE would fit in with the word EVE, when the voice came over the car radio.

"Car 15, Car 15. Come in," it announced. "The Governor requests that you deliver Miss Pickerell and friends directly to the Square Toe weather station. A young TV writer there says to tell Miss Pickerell that 'the nation is waiting for her exclusive story!' "

16

On National TV

Miss Pickerell sat back in the car dazedly. She had forgotten all about the young man and his "deal."

"Looks like you're going to be on TV coast to coast," said the Sheriff.

"Can I be on TV, too?" asked Euphus.

"I think so," said Miss Pickerell. "You're the only one who can explain about the laser beam."

"Me, on national TV," shouted Euphus, and he let out a long, loud whistle.

As soon as the car pulled up to the weather station, Mr. Humwhistel turned white. "Look!" he gasped. "Those television people have practically turned the weather station upside down.''

Miss Pickerell could see that they had. The long lobby had been converted into an auditorium. Rows of seats faced the reception desk where she had last seen the young woman with the waist-length hair and the purple-tinted spectacles. All except the first two rows were occupied. These had a RESERVED sign on them. The reception desk was nearly covered with microphones. A monitor set with a blank television screen stood at its left. Practically touching the desk on the right were six box-shaped computers, all with horizontal lines of colored lights that kept blinking on and off. They made Miss Pickerell a little dizzy.

"How could they have done this without consulting me?'' Mr. Humwhistel complained. "Computers are very sensitive instruments. They need to be handled with care.''

Miss Pickerell couldn't agree more. If machines were expected to do important things, she reflected, they had to be treated with respect. She said as much to Mr. Humwhistel as they watched a television crewman remove the door to the outer space communications system.

"There's a great deal of cable around," Miss Pickerell commented. The Governor had just spotted her and was carefully stepping over the heavy coils in an effort to reach her.

"I'm sure my equipment here will never be the same," Mr. Humwhistel exclaimed. "Come, Miss Pickerell. I'd better escort you to your seat."

The Governor took one arm, Mr. Humwhistel took the other, and together they guided her to the reception desk.

"Miss Pickerell." The young TV writer, who was standing there, reached out to shake her hand. "We've been waiting for you," he said, and grinned. "Please take your place behind the desk. You sit between Euphus and the Governor. The Governor's wife is on his other side. Oh, and we have a surprise for you!"

Miss Pickerell sat down. A battery of cameras, arranged in a semi-circle, shone on the reception desk area with dazzling intensity. They were hot and glaring. The TV writer motioned with his arms, and one of the crewmen brought the lamb and placed it on Miss Pickerell's lap. The lamb bleated uncomfortably.

"When does the show start?" Miss Pickerell asked.

6"Very soon! Very soon!" the TV man said, and he went over to the Governor and told him to stand up. "Watch the clock at the other end of the room. It is now 8:29," the young man explained. "In exactly sixty seconds we'll go on the air. A red light will also appear on the TV camera. That's your signal to begin."

"Act natural," the Governor's wife whispered to him, as he stood up.

Miss Pickerell watched the clock. When the second hand had moved three quarters of the way around the clock, the Governor cleared his throat. At 8:30, precisely when the red signal went on, he said, "Ladies and gentlemen."

The audience burst into applause. The cameras took pictures of the people clapping. Miss Pickerell had a chance to observe how crowded the weather station lobby was. She was glad to see that she knew most of the people in the audience. It made her feel much less nervous. She also noticed that her oldest niece, Rosemary, was sitting in the front row and that she had Pumpkins with her. He looked calmly into the cameras when they focused on him.

"Ladies and gentlemen," the Governor went on, "I am not going to make any speeches today. I will say only that this is a profoundly happy occasion for all of us. The lady who saved Square Toe County and made this happiness possible for us is Miss Lavinia . . ."

The audience rose in tribute to Miss Pickerell. She bowed and said, "Thank you all."

"I was most privileged to share some of her experiences with her," the Governor continued when the audience sat down. "So were a number of other people. Each one of us will tell part of the story. First, ladies and gentlemen, the eminent scientist in charge of our weather computers, Mr. Adrian Humwhistel!"

The Governor turned around to greet him. But Mr. Humwhistel was not there. The Governor looked questioningly at his wife. She smiled. He smiled, too.

"Well, ladies and gentlemen," he said, turning back to the audience, "this show is going to be more informal than I thought. Has anyone seen Mr. Humwhistel?''

The cameras focused on the audience again. Miss Pickerell gasped when they reached the last row and she saw her cow, guarded on one side by Mr. Kettelson and, on the other, by Mr. Humwhistel, standing in the aisle. Everybody laughed and clapped and Mr. Humwhistel came forward.

"Thank you! Thank you!" he said, when he faced the microphones. He explained that he had gone over to say "Hello" to Miss Pickerell's cow because he had not seen her in quite a while. Then he talked about the way weather computers normally worked. Miss Pickerell was very interested in what he had to say, particularly at the times when he used the computers to demonstrate exactly what he meant. She decided that she would probably feel much friendlier toward computers if she got to know them better.

"But, ladies and gentlemen," the Governor said, when Mr. Humwhistel finished, "there came a day when the weather computers were not functioning normally and our Square Toe County communications system with outer space broke down. On that day . . ."

The Governor showed Mr. Humwhistel's communications console. He introduced all the scientists at the weather station and then his wife and Deputy Administrator Blakely and Mr. Esticott and Mr. Kettelson. Miss Pickerell thought that she had never sat through such a long program. The lamb had fallen asleep. Miss Pickerell wished she could do the same.

At last, it was Euphus' turn. He spoke very clearly.

"You see," he explained, "the weather satellite was having trouble *only* over Square Toe County. That's why none of the scientists on the space station knew about it. A laser beam is a very hard thing to see because it's so narrow. But it is very powerful. Powerful enough to mix up a satellite 250 miles out in space." All of Square Toe County clapped when he finished telling about how he had figured out the connection between the giant laser at the new observatory and the blinding light. Miss Pickerell felt very proud of him.

"And now . . . ," the Governor began.

161

"Forevermore!" Miss Pickerell breathed, as two space-suited figures walked down the aisle.

"Ladies and gentlemen," the Governor shouted above the screams of the audience. "Professor Aceworthy, in charge of our weather department on the space station! And Terence, who gave Miss Pickerell the lamb! They will say just a few words."

Professor Aceworthy spoke with great sincerity about Miss Pickerell's resolve to do absolutely anything to spare the people of Square Toe County the miseries of another flood. Terence spoke with deep feeling about her love for all animals. The applause was deafening.

"And finally, ladies and gentlemen," the Governor called out, trying desperately to make himself heard, "Miss Lavinia Pickerell!"

Miss Pickerell handed the lamb, who was bleating again, over to Terence and got up. The Governor led her farther forward. She stood right next to the first blinking computer.

"There really isn't very much left for me to say," Miss Pickerell started. "The

Governor and Mr. Humwhistel and Euphus and all the rest of the speakers have
told you the facts. Being up on the weather
satellite was very exciting. But I find a lot
of other things exciting, too."

She paused and took a deep breath.

"I'll tell you about some of them," she
said. "I saw the swallows lined up on the
highway telephone wires on my way to the
weather station earlier today. The summer
in Square Toe County is coming to an end.
Some of the swallows were making up their
minds to leave for their long journey to the
south. I listened to the whistling of their
wings as they flew past me in flocks of a
dozen or more. A few jays and crows were
already flying in to take their place. And
I could almost smell the faint scent of gold-
enrods and river grapes on the air. I found
all of that very exciting."

Miss Pickerell paused again. The audience was very still.

"I wish I were a scholar like Mr. Humwhistel and Professor Aceworthy . . . ,"
Miss Pickerell began.

The audience applauded. Mr. Humwhistel and Professor Aceworthy waved.

"I was going to say," Miss Pickerell

went on, "that I can't really explain in the way I'm sure they could *why* I feel good when my cat, Pumpkins, purrs or when my cow moos contentedly or when Mr. Kettelson's face lights up with joy because he has some good news to tell me. . . ."

Miss Pickerell turned around. She thought she heard something. She was right. The lady reporter was choking back her tears. The people of Square Toe Mountain were drying their eyes with their handkerchiefs, too.

"I didn't mean to make anybody cry," Miss Pickerell said instantly. "I just wanted to explain that everything can be an exciting adventure and that we should all be very happy here on Earth. And now, I really must go home."

The audience cheered and clapped and shouted, "Bravo! Hurray!" The cameras swung around and around, taking as many pictures as they could. Miss Pickerell did not pay much attention. She was too busy trying to soothe the baby lamb.

ABOUT THE AUTHORS
AND ILLUSTRATOR

ELLEN MACGREGOR was born in Baltimore, Maryland. She created Miss Pickerell in the early 1950s and wrote four stories about her, as well as boxes full of notes for future adventures. She died in 1954, and not until 1964, after a long search, did Miss P. finally find Dora Pantell.

DORA PANTELL has been writing "something" for as long as she can remember—magazine stories, scripts for radio and television, and books for all ages. Ms. Pantell does her writing in lots of places, including airplanes and dentists' waiting rooms. She says that she most enjoys writing the Miss Pickerell adventures. There are now twelve titles in the series, all available in Archway Paperback editions.

Among Ms. Pantell's pastimes are reading nonviolent detective stories and listening to classical music. She lives in New York City with her three cats, Haiku Darling, Eliza Doolittle and Cluny Brown.

CHARLES GEER is an author as well as an artist, and has illustrated more books than he can count. He enjoys hiking, camping and sailing, and lives near Flemington, New Jersey with his wife, four children and a cat.

29990 THE GREATEST MONSTERS IN THE WORLD, by Daniel Cohen. Illustrated with reproductions and photographs. The intriguing pros and cons of the existence of Bigfoot, Nessie, the Yeti, and many other possible and impossible monsters. ($1.50)

29817 FOG MAGIC, by Julia L. Sauer. Illustrated by Lynd Ward. When Greta walks through the fog, she starts off on an adventure that takes her back to the past of one hundred years ago. ($1.25)

29948 BASIL OF BAKER STREET, by Eve Titus. Illustrated by Paul Galdone. The Mystery of the Missing Twins was one of the strangest and most baffling cases in the famous career of Basil—Sherlock Holmes of the mouse world. ($1.50)

29866 BASIL AND THE PYGMY CATS, by Eve Titus. Illustrated by Paul Galdone. Follow Basil to the mysterious East in one of the most perplexing cases of his famed career as the Sherlock Holmes of the mouse community. ($1.25)